Fly Toward Death

Fly Toward Death

Sally Laughlin

Prologue

An emergency meeting was called by the high-ranking officers of the Soviet Union after the surprise military attack by Germany on June 22, 1941.

The Soviet Union was unprepared for the onslaught the Germans were throwing at them on the ground and in the air.

A long wooden table with several chairs on each side and one at the head of the table dominated the austere room. Men in dark-green military uniforms brightened by gold, red or blue trim indicating their status shuffled through mounds of papers. They began addressing their government's weak air force strength, caused by the devastating air strikes that wiped out almost half of their air defense.

A general flipped to another page from the myriad papers in front of him and began reading it. He stopped and shook his head. "What is this nonsense? A petition for women who want to enter the war as pilots and soldiers? Why is this even on our table for discussion?"

Another general showed his scorn, "What is wrong with these women? They should stay at home in the kitchen, have children, and support our men."

"They do not have the physical or mental stamina it takes to fight a war like a man. They would die almost immediately." The first general said leaning forward on the table.

There was quiet in the room as all the generals looked toward the leader of the Soviet Union, Iosif Vissarionovich Stalin, sitting at the head of the table.

Stalin spoke firmly, "I had thought that at first, but I believe if these women wish to join the military and fight it might be to our advantage. We can train the women quickly, and it will free up the time for us to train our male pilots and soldiers better. This is an acceptable cost of war."

Chapter 1

Senior Lieutenant Vera Zhkov continually weaved her Biplane from the darkened sky into the bright search lights from below and back into the safety of the black shadows of the night. Machine-gun fire and rifle bullets zinged all around her as she maneuvered to drop her two bombs. Her fragile, two-seated, World War I Biplane was flying low enough for her to hear the Germans screaming and yelling as she pressed forward to her drop zone.

A shell from anti-aircraft cannons ripped through both wings of the plane; passing through to explode above her. The air was hard to breathe as the smoke from the discharged cannon filled her lungs and burned her eyes. The concussion from the blast caused her plane to be pushed downward, closer to the enemy below. Seconds later, bullets from a machine gun struck her plane just missing her engine and fuel line.

Vera raised her hand and her navigator, sitting behind her, grabbed the release lever and pulled hard. The two bombs attached to the belly of their plane fell downward hitting their target.

Quickly, Vera turned her plane from the glaring search lights, made a wide circle, and headed back to her airfield. Her hands and legs trembled as she fought to keep their shot-up plane in the air. "Are you all right?" Vera called back to her navigator.

"Flak went straight through our wings. No structural damage though." Lt. Ksenia Yivoskov, her navigator, leaned forward and yelled to Vera. "Did you get hit?"

"No, I am okay. Are you all right?" Vera asked again.

"If I could stop shaking, I could check me out," she said. "It appears that I am alright, but someone shot a hole in my pillow. Almost got me that time," Ksenia poked a finger through the large hole on the edge of the pillow she sat on.

"This was our fourth sortie," Vera said wiping the frost off her goggles. "We made it through this one alive. I hope it continues through the rest of the night."

"Through the rest of the night?" Ksenia blurted sardonically. "How about the rest of the war?"

* * *

TWO WEEKS EARLIER

Soldiers loaded the women into the back of the military truck and tied down the canvas covering that was whipping about in the cold, pelting rain. A soldier slapped the side of the driver's door, and the truck jerked and lurched as it began to move forward. A convoy of five trucks pulled away from the training base and headed out toward Stalingrad. Each truck held ten newly trained women pilots, navigators, mechanics, and armorers.

Vera Zhkov was an officer in the regiment and promoted to Senior Lieutenant because of her excellent flying skills during training. She sat in one of the military trucks and peered out at the disappearing city landscape through the canvas covering that offered little reprieve from the cold, wet winds.

Her large, blue-gray eyes looked around at the women in the truck. Vera's long, light brown hair was done up in a neat, tight bun at the back of her head. She glanced at each one of the women and realized she was the only one who had her hair tucked back. The rest of the girls had their long hair down. She knew they had fussed and primped so that the men would see them at their womanly best.

Vera sat back studying the young women she was traveling with in the very uncomfortable, cold military vehicle. Through the course of their army training as pilots, navigators, mechanics and ground crews, she came to know some of them quite well.

She was the oldest woman in this regiment at twenty-three years old, and the youngest was seventeen.

As far as Vera could tell, the young women were from universities, collective farms, factories, and stores where they worked as clerks.

The frigid and bumpy ride to the train station did nothing to deter the women in the truck from laughing and joking with each other.

Vera listened as they talked about all the handsome men in the army they had already encountered.

"I have never seen so many men in one place in all my life," a cherub-faced young girl giggled.

"Just think we are going to be surrounded by hundreds of men every day," another sighed. "We can dance and party all we want."

All the girls giggled and began telling stories about their home life before they became soldiers in the Red Army: All, except one.

Vera looked at the pensive, young woman sitting across from her at the end of the truck. Senior Lieutenant Elena Petrovka was nineteen, a petite and very bright woman. Throughout her pilot training, Elena excelled in every aspect of flying. Vera thought she was quite beautiful with her long, flaxen, blond hair and deep, blue eyes. And, her delicate features belied the fierce determination that drove her.

Vera was the only one who knew Elena's story. She looked out the slit from the canvas covering to the bleak landscape they were traveling through. Vera remembered the two of them talking quietly one night as they took a short break and walked around the training compound in Engels.

Elena's father was arrested as a traitor to the Soviet Union and shot for treason when she was fifteen years old. She knew he was not a traitor, and she was going to show them that the Petrovka name was an honorable, loyal name to the Soviet Union.

Vera had her own reasons for joining the Red Army Air Division. She thought back to that day on June 22, 1941 – a day she would never forget. She was staying with a friend near her younger brother's Army flight school and decided to visit him before she returned to the University. The only time he could see her was before his classes, so she got there early in the morning.

She had almost burst with pride as her brother walked toward her in his army uniform. "You look so handsome," she said. Sergei turned slowly around so she could admire him, and they broke out laughing.

They laughed and talked for a while until someone came running up to them telling them that the Germans had declared war on the Motherland. They had destroyed airfields, and they needed to get everyone in the air as fast as they could to stop the German Luftwaffe headed toward Moscow.

Vera was stunned. She protested saying that her brother had less than two months of training. She watched in shock as the young, inexperienced pilots raced past her toward their training planes. Sergei gave her a quick hug and took off with the rest of the students. Etched in her memory forever was her brother stopping, turning around, and waving at her with a big grin on his face. That was the last time she ever saw him. He was killed that day in an air battle over a barren field near Moscow.

* * *

The truck hit a large hole in the road jarring Vera's reverie back to the present. It was a long drive to Stalingrad from Engel's flight training academy. She thought they would have gotten there sooner, but the soldiers driving the military trucks, kept stopping frequently for the women to get out and do their private business. Vera knew the real reason was because they like flirting with all the young girls they were hauling to the train station.

Once they reached the train station all fifty women were crammed into two railway cars, along with the soldiers and civilians alike. Hours later, they finally reached their destination, which was a little village south of Moscow.

Every building in the village that had not been destroyed by the Germans was taken over by the Red Army. Most of the buildings were used to billet the soldiers and officers. One was used as a mess hall, another as a supply station, and a large house standing on the outskirts of the village was where the women were going to be temporarily billeted.

The women were advised to go to the supply station first to get their military uniforms. They were each issued a military jacket, a pair of pants and boots.

"What is this?" Elena held up the large, men-sized clothing and boots. "There is enough room for two people in these things."

"This is what you are issued," said the supply officer disgustedly as he handed out their uniforms.

Vera studied the short, balding, older man and wondered why he was just a corporal at his age.

"Do not blame me that they are letting women in the Army. The last bunch of females who came through here were digging dugouts for our real soldiers, complaining that their poor little hands were bleeding from using rough handled shovels. They had the nerve to ask me if I had any bandages or supplies to take care of their silly wounds."

"Did you have the bandages and medicine to accommodate these women?" Vera's voice held back the contempt she felt for this ignorant little man.

"Of course, I did. I told them I had bandages and ointments, but they were only for men who were doing the real fighting," he said emphasizing the word 'real.' He arrogantly looked at her up and down with disdain.

Vera straightened her back. Her voice rang of authority. "Comrade Corporal, are you as stupid as you look?"

"Yes, yes he is," a woman yelled from behind her.

"You will address me as Comrade Senior Lieutenant Zhkov," she leaned forward her eyes narrowed as she pointed to the display of bars and badges on her jacket. "If you ever, ever forget that again," she growled at him, "I will have you sent to Siberia for the rest of your life. If I find out that you have withheld bandages, medicines or anything else from any woman in the Red Army, in any way, I will personally come back here and shoot you between the eyes. And, I have spies everywhere, so do not think I will not find out."

Terror filled the man's eyes. He stepped back away from the fierce look Vera was throwing at him; his mouth open and eyes wide with fear.

"Now, finish giving out the uniforms' Comrade Corporal," Vera said with venom dripping from her words.

"Yes, Comrade Senior Lieutenant Zhkov," he said nervously grabbing jackets and other men-issue clothing, along with a gun and holster, to the rest of the women. After the last woman received her clothing he said, "You have all that you women were issued. That is it, Comrade Senior Lieutenant." His voice dripped with sarcasm.

He turned his face away, but not before Vera caught the sly smile he tried to hide.

Vera was the last one to receive her men's issue of clothing. She placed her clothing items on the top of his wooden counter, took her gun from its holster and placed it down on the countertop. "I believe there is more, Comrade Corporal." She said it so steely cold that he stumbled backward a couple of steps. Her menacing body language, her gun on the countertop, and her eyes filled with a deadly stare were not missed by him.

"Oh, yes, I forgot, Comrade Senior Lieutenant. Everyone is to receive bedding, too." He said hurrying into another area of the room.

Vera picked up her gun, replaced it in her holster, and snapped it closed. "Just wanted to see how heavy my gun was," she said, pretending that was the reason she had put her gun on the counter.

Everyone started to laugh. Vera gave them the signal to stop as the corporal came out of the storage room loaded down with blankets, pillows and thin mattresses. All the women quickly presented a serious face to the flustered supply officer, except for a couple of giggles somewhere in the group.

Finally, after the corporal had made several trips to the storage room, Vera and the others received all their military issue items.

The women placed everything neatly in a stack on top of their folded mattress, so they could carry it to their quarters without dropping anything on the muddy ground and headed out of the supply station.

On the way to the house where they were to be billeted, one of the women ran up to Vera, "Comrade Senior Lieutenant Zhkov that was wonderful. Would you come back and shoot him? Do you really have spies everywhere?"

"No on both counts, but I would like to think I could. Anyway, I would have thought of something to get him arrested." Vera laughed along with the other woman. "I have a feeling he is not going to be the first man to treat us as unworthy and unfit to serve in the Red Army."

"Speaking of 'unfit'," Elena said walking next to Vera. "How on earth are we supposed to fit into these?" She asked struggling with carrying her oversized military uniform and bedding.

"I was a seamstress before I was sent to the university. I think we can alter our uniforms so that they will not fall off us or hinder our performance," a tall, thin woman said walking behind Elena and Vera. Her large frame would easily fit into the men's uniform, so she would not have to alter her uniform too much. "I am Corporal Lubova Drukova, Soviet navigator. I will show you all how to do this," she smiled, and her small gray eyes lit up. Then, she looked down at the large boots issued to everyone. "Unfortunately, I am not a shoe cobbler, and I cannot fix the boots. However, if we stuff the tips of our boots with cloth or paper, we will be able to walk in them."

"Look at this," one of the women said aghast. "Look at this open flap in the front of the pants. There are no buttons to close it."

"That will be an easy fix," she sighed. "But, not so easy will be fixing the jackets and pants. You will all have to take out your sewing kits. We are going to have a lot of work to do."

The women walked into their temporary quarters and found bunk beds crammed into the small space of the house. A large fireplace had a fire blazing inside of it taking the edge off the bitter cold. Thin wooden slats were nailed over the broken windows but did little to keep the cold air from seeping in. The women picked their own bed and dropped everything on top of it.

Soon, all the women were getting tips and pointers from Lubova on how to cut down and fix their oversized uniforms. They worked by the light of the fireplace, and the four kerosene lanterns spaced strategically around the room. Hours later, they finished the last of the alterations and fell backward on their cots and fell asleep.

Early the next morning, the women were awakened and ordered to dress and report to their commanding officer outside. They dressed quickly and filed out of the house and were told to stand at attention while a ranking female officer addressed them. "I am Comrade Senior Captain Voskolov, your commanding officer. It has been reported that an army corporal in the supply unit was threatened by a female officer. He was so flustered he forgot the officer's name. The one who did this will step forward."

As Vera stepped forward so did every officer in their unit. Then, the lower-ranking women soldiers stepped forward as well.

"I see," the captain turned her head for a moment so that no one could see the smile that was trying to escape. She turned back and looked sternly at the women in front of her. "It was brought to my attention that he was threatened to be sent to Siberia and a bullet to the head. Is that correct?"

Every woman replied at the same time, "Yes, Comrade Senior Captain."

"When I asked him why he was threatened he said he had no idea why this officer would threaten him. He was just doing his duty."

She walked up and down the line of women standing at attention, "I questioned him further, and it came out that he had said something about his refusing to help treat the hands of the useless women who came through here yesterday; the women who had been digging dugout shelters for the male soldiers." The captain stopped in front of Vera. "He is just a sample of what we, as women soldiers, are going to have to endure, until we can show them our skills and dedication are worthy of their best male soldiers." The captain stood for a moment in silence and began again. "I cannot punish the entire regiment, so I will forget this incident. The corporal, for his actions, is being sent to the front lines. However, refrain from threatening any more incompetent, unintelligent soldiers." She waited for a moment and added, "Is that clear?"

In unison, they responded, "Yes, Comrade Senior Captain Voskolov."

Vera studied the captain standing before them. She was not especially pretty, and her very short, light-brown hair did nothing to add to her physical presence. And then Vera was stunned by the next thing the captain ordered.

"You women are in the Red Army as soldiers." She began walking up and down the line of women standing at attention and stopped in front of Elena. "You will all report to the army barber. All of you must cut your hair so that you look like a soldier and not a primping woman."

There was an audible gasp from the women. Vera knew their long hair was their pride and joy.

The captain shrugged and said, "You can either cut your own hair or go to the army barber. It is up to you, but he does cut the hair very, very short. Your hair should not touch your shoulders. Those who disregard this order will be put in the guard house for two weeks, and then sent to the Army barber. You are dismissed."

Almost all the women walked somberly back to their quarters, except for a couple of the women who felt short hair would be great to have and elected to go to the army barber.

An hour later, the floor of their house was filled with long locks in various lengths and colors. They all sat somberly and watched as their hair was swept up and thrown into the fireplace.

Vera looked around at the sad faces of the women and said, "We volunteered to help get the fascists out of our country. This is a small sacrifice." She fluffed her short hair, "It will be all right. Our hair will grow back after the war."

She looked over at Elena, who just sat on her bed staring at the long, luxurious hair of hers being swept up and thrown into the fire. "It took me nineteen years to get it that long," she sighed. "I will be an old lady by the time it grows to that length again."

"Let us hope we all live through this war and can grow our hair long again," Vera said softly to herself.

"Lt. Ksenia Yivoskov, navigator here. Actually," Ksenia said, playing with her new short hairdo. "I like it. It's not pulling on my head anymore. And, it will be easier to maintain." She flipped her light, brown hair around her face. Her small, brown eyes sparkled slightly in her pudgy face.

"Well, I am glad someone is happy," Vera laughed and mimicked Ksenia's flipping her hair around her face.

Everyone laughed, except Elena.

The next morning the women were called for a meeting with Senior Captain Voskolov. "Your planes will arrive tomorrow morning. There was a terrible snowstorm, and they had to wait until it blew over. Pilots and navigators, you will be able to test them tomorrow to make sure they are working properly to your specifications. After all, the planes will be adjusted to the men who will be flying them in, and you want to make sure you can reach everything in the cockpits."

After their briefing, the women walked back to their quarters. One of the women began to sing a song. Her voice was so beautiful that, even though it was a rousing song, they all let her sing it alone. Afterward, they had her sing in their quarters, and soon another woman began harmonizing with her, and there wasn't a dry eye in the house when they sang a soulful song of love, and love lost.

Then, Lieutenant Natalya Mykolina began reciting poems. Her pretty face lit up as she recited one poem after another. Sometimes she had everyone laughing and at times tears ran down their faces as they listened to poems of love, life and death.

Later that day, after they had eaten their dinners and were in their quarters, one of the women came running into the house excitedly. "We have all been invited to a dance," she blurted out.

"A dance?" One of the women jumped up off her bed. "Did you say a dance?"

"Yes," she giggled. "The men have moved all the tables in the mess hall and have brought in a record player. They are waiting for us."

"Oh, that is wonderful," one of the women began twirling about the room.

"Yes, wonderful," Natalya said. "I need a mirror, so I can fix my hair."

"What hair?" Ksenia asked.

"Oh," Natalya said realizing her hair was now short. "Oh," she said again with a great deal of sadness.

"Come on," Ksenia laughed. "I wish I looked as lovely as some of you with such short hair. Besides, do you think they are going to care? After all, we are women."

It didn't take any of the women long to hurry to the mess hall. They were not disappointed as the hall was crowded with so many soldiers they could hardly move.

Flirting was running rampant and Vera noticed that even Elena was having a good time. In spite of her shortened hair, there were so many men around Elena, she could barely see her.

The whole night was filled with laughter and dancing, but all too soon they had to call it a night.

Almost the entire male regiment walked the women back to their quarters. A few kisses and hugs here and there, and the women entered their quarters and shut the door on the enamored soldiers standing outside.

Chapter 2

Morning came quickly for the tired women as they were awakened early enough to grab their breakfast before they reported to the airfield at 0600 hours.

Vera and Elena were greeted by Private Ulyana Ubuchova, one of the kitchen helpers, with a hot cup of coffee as they sat down on one of the long, wooden benches in the mess hall.

"Your planes have arrived," Ulyana said cheerfully. Her short, light brown hair hung straight around her face, making her look even thinner than she already appeared. She was the youngest and tallest girl in the regiment, and Vera thought, probably the thinnest, too.

"Yes, we saw them on the way here," Vera tried to sound awake and as cheerful as Ulyana, but she didn't quite make it.

"Now starts what we were trained for," Elena said excitedly as she took a piece of bread from one of the baskets sitting on the table.

Vera looked at her friend's face, which was alive with excitement, but she could not match her enthusiasm. "Yes," she said, "Now it starts."

Their U2 Biplanes lined the edge of the field like giant dragon flies. They had been flown in and parked off the field to the side so they would not interfere with the takeoff and landing of the bomber and fighter planes already on the airfield.

After a lengthy briefing, the women walked briskly toward their U2 World War I Biplanes. A U2 was what they trained in, and everyone was very familiar with how this plane functioned. They had no radios for communication, and no cannons or machine guns to protect themselves. The U2 plane was made of the thinnest material; canvas and plywood, and the only metal on the plane was the engine, the throttle stick and the steel rods that supported the fixed wheels.

Each pilot, navigator and mechanic were assigned to a specific plane.

"Comrade Elena," Vera turned looking at the petite woman walking next to her as they approached their own planes. "I thought that was a very good suggestion to cut our engines and glide in before we dropped our bombs."

"I do not think this base commander liked my adding my opinion," Elena shrugged. "He wants a demonstration before we take off for our new airfield."

"Alright," Vera smiled. "We know what this little U2 can do. So, we will show him together."

"We are going to be like bees in pants to the sleeping fascists," Elena said smiling up at Vera. "Harassment missions have never been done before. I do believe it will be effective in demoralizing the enemy as well, like Senior Captain Voskolov said."

"Yes, I believe that, too." Vera glanced around at the young women pilots, navigators and mechanics; all of them seemed excited as they began checking out their planes. "But they are all so young. This is war, not a party like they have had the last few months. It is serious."

"Yes, comrade," Elena nodded. "They have not met the horrors that come with war."

"Have you?" Vera questioned curiously.

"Yes," Elena stopped in front of her plane. "I went on a recon mission once with one of our instructors. We spotted a town that was pounded down into the ground; flattened for miles and miles."

"A whole town?"

"Yes, the whole town had been pulverized into a crumbled mass of brick and stone."

Elena was quiet for a moment and then spoke again. "Even worse, we flew over a battlefield, and I saw bodies of our troops and the fascists strewn about like grotesque broken dolls." She paused again and shook her head almost as if she was trying to get the image out of her head. "The instructor and I did not speak all the way back. We were both sickened by what we saw. War is ugly. I hate war. I hate killing. I only want to rid our country of the invading fascists and get back to peace."

"You have spoken what I believe as well. All right," Vera said. "Let us show him what we can do, and then we can get to our new base and get rid of the fascists as soon as we can."

Vera and Elena had their planes checked by their mechanics to make sure that they had been refueled and were in perfect condition.

Elena led the way as they taxied down the airfield field and took off into the gray skies.

Following behind the two women were two fighter pilots whom the base commander had ordered to protect the women if needed, and he wanted his own eyewitnesses to the event. He was not quiet about his feelings and let everyone know that he expected the planes and the women flying them to fail.

They climbed to 6000 feet, and then Elena brought her plane down to 3000 feet, shut her engines off, and began to glide.

Vera followed Elena, mirroring her every step of the way.

Soon, Elena dropped down to 800 feet and glided for a couple of miles until she was directly over the base, and then started her engines. She pulled on the throttle and made a hard right. Both women made a wide circle and lined up to land on the runway. When they landed, they were met with a rousing cheer from their squadron and even some of the male regiments.

The base commander confirmed with his pilots, that had flown behind Vera and Elena, the little Biplane could indeed cut its engine, glide in, and fly low enough to drop its bombs and then restart its engines in mid-air.

Shortly after they had landed all the women pilots, and navigators were told to report to the command center for a briefing on their flight patterns before they flew out to their new base.

All the other women, who were the ground crews, were ordered to ride in a military truck to their new airfield. There were a lot of hugs and tears as the soldiers at the base came to wish them luck. The women climbed into the trucks and headed away from the base.

Their base was only about twenty miles from the one they just left. After a long, uncomfortable ride, they were taken to a wide, expansive, grassy field and dropped off. They stood there, in complete confusion, looking at the open field in front of them.

"So, where are the houses?" Ulyana asked. "Where are we going to sleep?"

The little puttering of the U2's could be heard heading for the women standing near the airfield. They watched and waited until the pilots, and navigators landed, grabbed their belongings and walked toward them.

"Why are we here?" One of the women asked looking at the open field with no visible housing anywhere in sight.

Just then Captain Voskolov appeared from around a mound of stones and walked over to the women. "That was perfect timing. Ground crews listen up. Drop your bedding and other non-essential items in your quarters, and report immediately to your designated plane and have it ready for the pilots and navigators to take off. Pilots and navigators do the same, except report to base headquarters. Come I will show you where your quarters are located. Follow me."

She led them around a pile of stones and dirt where a canvas cloth hung in front of an opening, and with a sweep of her hand moved the canvas cloth. "These are your new quarters until further notice."

The women stood with disbelief etched on their faces. Their new quarters were nothing more than dugouts in the ground. Stones and mud were built up to create a portico-like structure, and a heavy sheet of canvas hung in front of each dugout as a door covering. A total of seven dugouts that could house ten women in each one had been built. One of the dugouts had been dedicated to the captain and higher-ranking officers and doubled as the base command center. Another dugout housed all their fuel, weapons and ammunition.

The women were informed into which group they fell and filed into their prospective dugouts.

All ground crews were quartered together, as were all pilots and navigators. Everyone knew where they were going by the list the captain had given them, except Ulyana. She followed Vera and her group into their dugout.

The dugouts were cold, damp and smelled of wet earth and mildew. Inside each of the women's dugouts were ten small beds made of wood planks. A weathered, kerosene heater stood in the middle of the room barren of any heat. Vera shivered as the canvas door blew open letting in more of the bitter cold.

"Great, no heat. I always wanted a place like this. It is so down to earth," Ksenia remarked sarcastically.

Vera groaned and rolled her eyes, "Did you really just say that?"

Everyone laughed and began selecting their cots.

Natalya walked around the small room looking at the four dirt walls, "Say," she said. "Where are the toilets?"

"Oh, I saw it over by the edge of the trees," Ulyana piped up.

"Nothing we are not used to," Ksenia nodded.

Ulyana looked around at the small dugout and noticed there was not a cot for her to put her stuff down on. "There are not enough beds for me. What do I do?"

Vera took some of the things Ulyana held in her arms that were falling on the ground. "Comrade Ulyana, I am not sure where you are going to be quartered. I think you followed the wrong group." She smiled warmly at the young girl. "Go with us to the base commander's quarters. She will have your designated dugout."

Quickly, Natalya and Ksenia lit the kerosene heater and lamps. Cots were made up, and the few personal items they had were thrown on top of their beds.

All the crude shelters emptied as the mechanics and ground crews headed for their planes, and the pilots and navigators hurried to report to Captain Voskolov.

Inside the captain's quarters, a kerosene heater was going strong, although the room inside still felt damp and cold. Kerosene lamps were lit, and the twenty women were ushered in and told to stand around the table.

The captain did not waste any time in giving her orders for the night. "You will leave when the sun sets. You will glide in at 3000 feet, drop down to 800 feet, and cut your engines as you get closer to your target. When you see your target, you will drop your payloads, and return to base to be refueled and pick up two more bombs."

"How many times will we be doing this?" Natalya asked.

"Your sorties will begin when the sun sets and stops when the sun first starts to rise. We are going to wear the enemy down by bombing them every few minutes. They are about to have a lot of very sleepless nights. The mechanics and armament crews understand they will have to work quickly to get any damage done to your planes fixed, fueled and flight-ready so you will be in the air no less than five to ten minutes from landing. Understood?"

Everyone acknowledged they understood. "Good, I have also assigned the following pilots and navigators who will be flying together. The ground mechanics and armament personnel have already received their assigned plane." She handed each of the pilots and navigators a roster listing flight teams and their assigned ground crew.

"What about kitchen help? Are we assigned someone as well?" Ulyana asked. She, and two other women who would be working in the mess hall, had followed Vera and the other pilots and navigators because they were not told where to go either.

"Of course," she fumbled around the papers scattered on the wooden table, found what she was looking for, pulled it out, and handed it to one of the women. "Now, I want you all to become familiar with your new base. There is a quickly built wooden frame house that will be used as our mess hall. There is a toilet located outside away from our quarters. It will have to be shoveled out from time to time, but I will assign workers for that. You are dismissed."

Vera checked out the roster telling her who her navigator would be. She was delighted that Lt. Ksenia Yivoskov was going to be her navigator. They became very good friends at Engels during their training.

It was getting colder, and a heavy fog began to roll in as the women made their way to the wooden shanty that was their mess hall. Everyone was busy laughing and talking about who they were teamed up with; everyone except Elena.

Vera noticed the mood change in Elena. "Comrade Elena you do not seem so happy. Are you disappointed in your assigned crew?"

Elena jerked her head around as if she was hearing Vera for the first time, "No, no comrade. It is not that. It is just that I want to be a fighter pilot, not a bomber."

"Maybe they will see your great flying skills and promote you to a fighter plane," Ksenia said.

"I will prove to them that I deserve to fly a fighter plane," Elena's face showed signs of her immense determination. "I will. You will see."

"I am glad you are here with us now. You are a wonderful pilot," Vera said.

"I will work as a team with all of you, but my heart is somewhere else," Elena said with half a smile.

They finished their meal of cabbage soup, bread and coffee and were sitting around talking when Ksenia burst through the door of the mess hall.

"I was out having a cigarette when I saw our trucks coming back." Ksenia's eyes began to sparkle with excitement. "The truck drivers told me that the weather was so bad the pilots and crew members at our last base have been grounded. Fortunately for us, the ground is clear enough for the truck drivers to see. They said they will drive us to the base for another dance and bring us back before it gets dark." She spoke loudly so that all the women could hear her.

Excitement ran rampant in the mess hall. When the captain walked in an immediate hush fell over the women.

"What was all the excitement about?" the captain asked.

"We were told that all the pilots at our last base were grounded, and the ground crew was given the day off. The truck drivers said they could take us back to the base for a going-away dance and have us back here before dark, Comrade Commander Sr. Captain Voskolov." Ksenia spoke respectfully and quietly.

The captain stood there for a moment looking at all the hopeful faces peering at her. "Your flights have been canceled as well. I see no reason why you cannot enjoy yourselves one last time."

A deafening roar erupted from the women as they screamed and jumped around. They quickly saluted the captain and hurried past her out the door.

"I love being in the Army," one of the women said racing past the captain.

Elena stayed back for a moment, "That will all change too soon."

"Yes, fortunately they have no idea of the hell they have gotten themselves into. Go," the captain said, and motioned for Elena and Vera to leave.

"Thank you, Comrade Sr. Captain," they said and hurried after the women already climbing into the waiting trucks.

The captain walked over to the women serving the meals. "I can help myself. Go. Go and enjoy"

"Yes, Comrade Sr. Captain Voskolov," Ulyana squealed with delight. She and the two other young women working with her in the kitchen saluted the captain as they raced out the door screaming, "Wait for us."

* * *

By the next afternoon, the skies had cleared, and all the pilots and navigators were given their final flight path. "You will be dropping your payloads on a German tank division that is heading toward one of our railroad depots. They are about twenty miles from our military regiment that was sent to protect the railroad and are now blocked in by the German tank division advancing toward them."

"What type of bombs do we have against the tanks?" Vera asked.

"You will be carrying anti-tank bombs this time. The German high command knows it is an important supply line for us, and their mission is to cut if off and destroy it." She stood back and crossed her arms. A wry smiled crossed her face. "The fascists are a very neat army. They have helped you and do not even know it. They line their tents and equipment in very neat rows making them an easy target."

Night came, and the women hoisted themselves up on the wing of their plane and climbed into their respective open cockpits; pilot in the first cockpit, and navigator in the cockpit directly behind her.

The little rumble of their Biplane engine turned over as the ground mechanics rotated the propellers. One by one of the planes lifted off the ground in a single line and headed toward the German target shown on their maps.

Vera was grateful that Elena volunteered to be the lead plane, because there were no lights in the cockpits making it impossible to read the maps. During their training at Engels Vera noticed that Elena had an uncanny ability to survey the night landscape and match it up to the coordinates on the maps they were given.

It wasn't long before Vera saw Elena waggle her wings. That was Elena's clue that she had found the German forces. Vera waggled her wings and each pilot after her waggled their wings for the plane behind her to get ready to glide in and drop their bombs.

Elena cut her engines, and Vera did the same. They glided over the sleeping enemy with only the sound of the wind softly whining against the wire bracing and struts of the wings.

The quiet of the night was shattered when the first bomb hit a tank.

Vera was flying so low she could hear the shouts and screams from soldiers below. Bullets from rifle fire, machine guns and pistols whizzed all around her. Suddenly, search lights hit the sky accompanied by the ack-ack sound of the anti-aircraft cannons. But it was too late; the damage already was done. The women had dropped their payloads hitting several tanks and were now headed back to their airfield.

Their return to the base was marred. The once bright moonlight had become covered with thick clouds taking away any visibility of the landscape below. Vera struggled to find any land reference that might help her get back to the base. She looked over at Elena, who waggled her wings and banked a hard right. Vera thought she could see Elena waving for her to follow. She wasn't sure, but she followed her anyway.

So, like a mother duck with her little ducklings, everyone followed Elena in a single file.

They had been flying for a while, and Vera thought they were lost until she saw the flares from the ground crew shooting up in the sky showing them where to land. She was stunned. She could not figure out how Elena knew the right flight pattern to get them back to the base.

When all the planes landed safely and the pilots and navigators jumped to the ground, they joined the ground crews who were singing and dancing.

Sr. Capt. Voskolov was there on the field watching them. She called for all the pilots and navigators to join her in the base command center. "Congratulations, you all made it back here safely and all of your payloads were delivered. However, now you must be careful. They will be expecting you from this day forward."

"We have lost the element of surprise," Vera said.

"Yes, yes, you have." The captain thought for a moment before she spoke. "I think the next time we will plan the attack from a different direction. We still may have the advantage of surprise, for now."

"It is very dark this night and hard for the other pilots to find their way," Elena stated. "If we must use our flares, then I suggest that we use them wisely. The Germans will have doused all their lights and anything that might give away their location. We may need to drop a flare for us to see our targets."

"That will give them a location of where your planes are as well," the captain said.

"Unfortunately, if the clouds do not release the light of the moon, then it is what we must do, Comrade Sr. Captain," Vera said.

"So be it," the captain sighed. "Fly safely, comrades, fly safely. I would like to see all of your faces in the mess hall tomorrow afternoon."

Vera and the others raced to their planes. The mechanics had already loaded the second set of bombs for the night and refueled their planes.

The dark landscape below began to change as the clouds finally moved away from covering the moon. Vera was relieved that they did not have to drop their flares this evening, but she knew the time would come when she would have to use them.

Elena was lead again, with Vera right behind her. As they approached the enemy, they cut their engines and glided toward the target below. Elena dropped her bombs first, and suddenly the sky was filled with bright illuminations from the search lights below. And again, the bullets began whizzing around them from the weapons below.

Everyone made it back to the base safely, but some of the planes were badly damaged by bullets and flak. Vera landed and started to crawl out of her cockpit when she noticed a hole from a bullet that had ripped through the plane and exited through her cockpit seat. During all the excitement, and her fright, she didn't hear or feel it penetrate so close to her. It missed her by a couple of inches.

Even though no one was injured, and the jubilant ground crews were yelling and laughing, Vera found it hard to stop the trembling of her legs and body.

One of the pilots climbed out of her cockpit, scrambled to the ground and began heaving and gasping for air. Her navigator stood by her until the pilot was through and then reached down and gently helped her up.

Vera noticed that Elena seemed to be the only one of the flight crews who was not affected during their last sortie.

It wasn't until after their sixth sortie, when a thin line of light began to etch its way into the blackness of the night, the weary women landed their planes on their airfield.

"Well, that was a fun night," Ksenia said sarcastically as she took off her leather cap and walked toward her dugout with Vera.

"And just think, we get to do this over and over again every night," Vera replied mockingly. The smell of burning kerosene, grease and damp earth greeted her as she pulled back the canvas covering over their door. It was almost welcoming to her. Vera's legs were still shaking when she fell onto her bed with her clothes on. Sleep did not come easy as she tossed and turned until finally her eyes closed, and sleep crept over her.

Chapter 3

Vera longed for peace. They had been flying sorties for just two weeks, but it seemed like they had been doing it for years. Every day when darkness descended upon them, they got into their planes and dropped their payloads until the morning sun began to grasp its hold in the cold, shadowy sky.

Their sorties every night was becoming more and more dangerous, because the Germans forces were prepared. The element of surprise no longer existed.

Ksenia and Vera sat in their Biplane as the ground crew worked feverishly to patch up the holes in the wings, attach two more bombs to their plane, fueled it up, and checked out the plane as thoroughly as possible in the allotted time.

"Thanks for sitting with me." Ksenia placed her hands on her legs that were jerking about as she sat there. "There is no way I could have walked to the mess hall for a cup of coffee."

"My legs are doing the same thing, so it is no problem," Vera leaned her head forward to rest on the dashboard. "We had a couple of really close calls that last sortie."

The ground crew gave the thumbs up for the two women to begin their next, and seventh, sortie of the night. In the deep, dark of the night, they headed down the grassy runway and lifted off into the cloudless sky. In a single file, all the planes that could fly took off and headed back to their targets again.

It was a steady stream of U2 Biplanes coming in and flying out. It was like a giant loop. Planes taxied in to get fixed, fueled and loaded with two more bombs, and those planes taking off again to drop their new payloads.

Silently, Vera's small Biplane flew toward the German encampment. Her heart was racing the closer she got to the enemy. She was thankful that there was no moon shining that night making it easier to surprise the sleeping soldiers. On the other hand, it made it harder for them to find their target below.

Vera was angry they were not given radios or navigation devices. It would have made flying much easier for them; if she could call what they did easy.

She knew that Captain Voskolov kept trying to get more supplies and equipment for the all-women regiment, but it was always the same answer – we need it for the men fighting the war.

Vera looked down as they passed over a small, frozen lake. She remembered the lake from the last time they flew this mission about twenty minutes ago. She smiled and sighed with relief; their target was less than a mile ahead.

She reached over and shut off her engines. The only sound that broke the silence was the wind that slipped through some of the bullet holes in her plane, and the soft whine of the wind playing the wires of their wings like an eerie harp. Although, she could barely hear those sounds against the pounding of her heart as she approached their target. Her large blue-gray eyes strained to make out the attack zone below through the frosted goggles she wore.

Elena was over her target. Vera was second and glanced back at her comrade pilots as they all lined up behind her for their next drop. She hoped they would all make this drop safely. The search lights burst into the sky along with the screams of the men below, and the continuous fire of the machine guns, rifles and anti-aircraft fire. Vera dove in and out of the light, made her drop, and banked her plane away from the percussion of the bomb blast below and headed for home base.

Elena's plane landed safely, and she pulled her plane into her parking spot. But Vera was struggling trying to land her plane. Her landing was rough and the uneven terrain she had to land on didn't make it any easier. Finally, she got control of the shaking plane, eased back on the throttle and pulled her plane into its parking spot. She switched off the engines and dropped her head for a moment in relief.

She glanced up when Ksenia touched her shoulder and pointed to two planes coming in for a landing that seemed to be having problems. One plane landed hard and swerved off the runway. The other plane crash landed near the runway in an open field. Emergency trucks raced down the field toward the two planes.

Vera and Ksenia sat there watching helplessly as the badly wounded pilots and navigators were pulled from their planes. Everyone on the runway was silent for a moment until the other planes started flying in to have their planes repaired, fueled, and re-armed.

It was a long night for Vera and the others as they flew sorties until the sun began to peak through the night's black curtain.

The next night at their briefing, they were all given a new target, and its coordinates. They were all silent as they walked to their planes. There was no element of surprise anymore, and each sortie was more dangerous than the next.

Vera and Ksenia's plane took off and twenty minutes later she approached their new target, shut off her engine, dropped to the proper level, and glided in to discharge her payload.

Suddenly, brilliant search lights exploded up into the sky illuminating their planes. Anti-aircraft shells exploded all around her causing her plane to be jostled around and harder to control. Her eyes burned from the smoke, and the debris from the flack made it visibility harder to see the target below.

Bile rose up in Vera's throat as she positioned her plane over the enemy target below. Now!" she yelled and raised her hand signaling for Ksenia to release the bombs.

Ksenia pulled her goggles up to her forehead and leaned over the side of the Biplane, so she could get a better view of the drop site. Her hand was tightly gripped around the release lever. Assessing the right target below, she pulled the lever and the two bombs that were strapped to the belly of their U2 Biplane hurled downward toward their destination.

The screams and shouts from below were followed by the rat-ta-tat-tat of machine-gun fire amid the sound of pistol and rifle bullets that zinged close to her airplane. Anti-aircraft cannons with their tracing bullets were shooting steadily into the sky mixing in with the illumination from the bright search lights. For a fleeting second, Vera though it would have been a beautiful sight, if it hadn't been such a deadly one.

A brilliant flash near her in the air caused her to be blinded for a second. Then, in horror, she saw it was from one of the planes behind her that had burst into flames. She could hear the screams of the pilot and navigator as the flames engulfed them. Vera looked down and watched helplessly as the flaming plane hurled into the ground and exploded on impact.

A bullet went through her airplane just missing her leg. She maneuvered her plane upward and turned the engine back on. "Are you alright?" She called back to Ksenia.

"Yes," Ksenia said. "Are you all right?"

"Yes, but our plane is not. I hope we can make it back safely,"

Vera struggled to keep her bullet-ridden plane in the air. A long stream of dark smoke poured out of her plane, following her like a black rope of death. Bullet holes had ripped into the wings, along with a couple of larger holes from the anti-aircraft flak the Germans threw at them. There were so much smoke and powder in the air from the flak she could barely breathe and her eyes burned and were tearing up, making it difficult to see. Her plane wobbled and jerked in the air, as Vera struggled to keep it flying.

The planes headed back to base for another load of bombs. The blackness of the night made it almost impossible to see any landmarks causing great anxiety among the pilots.

Vera was getting worried until she saw the fire lit by the ground crew and the light of flares that smacked against the darkness of the night.

Vera approached the landing strip and tried to ease her plane to the ground. Instead, her plane hit the ground hard. The wheels under the plane groaned and creaked as the plane bounced and swerved slightly off course. With all her strength, Vera got the plane back onto the runway and braked to slow the plane down.

Struggling with the controls, Vera maneuvered her plane into her parking spot away from the other planes that were coming in directly behind; she shut off her engine. Her ground crew immediately began working on the plane, even before she got out of it.

One by one of the planes came in for a landing. A couple of planes pulled off at the edge of the field, smoke billowing from them. Ground crews raced toward the damaged planes and their wounded pilots and navigators. Ambulances sirens screamed as they raced to the end of the field where the injured women were being pulled from their planes.

The sound of a sputtering engine trying to come in for a landing drew everyone's attention. It was coming in to fast for it to land. "Too fast! Too fast! Pull up! Pull up!" Vera screamed. She watched in horror as the plane hit the ground, flipped over and exploded.

Everyone stood for a moment in shock, and then the tears came. Vera's her heart was heavy as the wounded were pulled from their planes, and at the loss of her friends killed in this last sortie.

In the darkness of a cold, damp night that surrounded her, Vera fought back the tears for her lost friends. Her lip quivered, and her body shook as she climbed down from her plane.

She looked at Ksenia and saw tears streaming down her face. They walked toward each other and embraced. Ksenia cried softly on Vera's shoulder. After a couple of minutes, Vera patted Ksenia's shoulder. "Come on, we need something to warm us up."

"This is shot up badly." Senior Sergeant Rimma Trovitz said. She was assigned to Vera and Ksenia's U2 Biplane as their mechanic and armament crew, along with Corporal Larissa Ivanovich. Both women were average height and build, but there was nothing average about their knowledge of the Biplane. Rimma interrupted Vera's emotional thoughts. "You managed to have the AA guns punch through the bottom and top wings. You two were very lucky this time."

"Yes, we were lucky this time," Vera said solemnly.

Larissa walked to the damaged wing of their plane and shook her head. "Now those are a lot of holes to patch up."

"Comrade Larissa, we have patched up worse than these," Rimma said as they began working on the bullet-ridden wings of the plane. Her small, green eyes narrowed slightly as she scanned the damage. "I hear the trucks' rolling," she yelled to Larissa.

The rumble of a truck grew closer as it traveled toward the edge on the grassy runway where it would wait until the mechanics, and armament crew arrived. The truck was loaded with the bombs that were to be installed under the Biplane's belly for the next run.

"Yeah," Larissa said. Her short, brown hair stuck out from under her leather cap. Her thin lips pressed together as she shook her head. "This has to be really tough for them. I hope they're strong enough to keep doing this."

"Well, she had better toughen up because a lot more of her friends are going to be flying, but not a plane, just with their angel wings."

"Now that was harsh," Larissa quipped.

"I know. But if I think about all this death and destruction, I will be sobbing all the time. Although, lately, I have been crying a lot at more as more of our friends don't return."

"Yeah, me, too," Larissa spoke sadly.

"Right now, we do what we can for them," Rimma reached over and patted Larissa's arm. "Did you check the lever to make sure it will work to release the bombs?"

"Hold on," Larissa climbed onto the wing. After carefully inspecting the release levers she called down to Rimma. "They are working fine. A couple of bullets just missed them." She said, as she jumped to the ground.

They walked to the truck at the end of the airfield that was loaded with bombs. They unloaded one of the two bombs they had to attach to the under-belly of the plane. "These things are heavy," Larissa grumbled more to herself than Rimma.

"We are going to have bigger muscles in our arms than a man," Rimma sighed as they carried it to the plane.

"We already have bigger brains than a man, why not muscles," Larissa said.

"I like your thinking, comrade," Rimma smiled as they reached their plane.

Quickly, they armed the bomb and then, both on their knees, attached the bomb to the straps that held the bomb underneath the plane. They repeated the same thing with the second bomb.

Larissa arched her aching back and moaned. "This will be their eighth air strike tonight."

"Yes," Rimma said rubbing her frozen hands together. "And the sky will not be light for a couple of hours. So, this will be a long night."

"For them and us," Larissa said checking under the plane one last time.

Rimma stood with her freezing hands on her hips, "I guess this little plane does the job for them."

"Sure, but they are still relics. These planes were used during World War I." Her hand gestured toward the other planes sitting on the makeshift runway.

"What can they do?" Rimma shrugged.

"I know. I know. But that does not make it right." Larissa said shaking her head. "From what I have heard and seen, they have to work and train harder than the men."

"Well, sure," Rimma gave a small laugh. "The men do not want women out-flying them. Although, I have heard of several women who are great flyers and can out-fly most of the male pilots."

"I know who you mean, our own Comrade Vera and that little girl, Comrade Elena. How did someone get to be that pretty?" Larissa said as she worked on replacing a shot-up panel on the wing.

"Unfair it is. Unfair indeed," Rimma said as she took down a damaged canvas panel from the underside of the plane and put another panel in its place. "Comrade Elena has beauty and brains and that little thing is fearless. I would be jealous of her, but she is so annoyingly nice, and I truly like her a lot."

"What are you talking about? You are not so bad on the eyes yourself." Larissa finished replacing the last panel on the wing and moved to check the rudder.

Rimma stopped and put her hands on her hips, "I think you are very pretty, too."

"Yeah, yeah," Larissa said. "Okay, I guess we are not so bad looking either. However, we are definitely not on Sr. Lt. Elena Petrovka's level."

"Who is?" Rimma asked.

A cold wind kicked up and nipped bitterly at their bare hands and faces as they worked feverishly to have the plane ready for Vera and Ksenia when they returned.

"My hands are getting numb," Larissa rubbed her hands and blew her hot breath on them.

"Some of the bases have hangers. It sure would be nice if we had a hanger to work on these planes." Rimma put her hands under her armpits to try to warm them up.

"What and stay out of the wind? You do not like working in an open field with all this fresh air?" Larissa blew one last time on her hands and started patching up the holes on the second wing. "Freezing and frost bite is just part of the exotic lure of being a mechanic," she said scrunching up her frozen face at Rimma.

"Open fields and no protection from the prevailing winds," Rimma took her freezing hands from under her armpits and shook them for a moment. "I used to help build aerodromes. If we had the time, I think I would start building one now." With a deep sigh, she moved to check the fuselage making sure it hadn't been too badly damaged. "A couple of bullets grazed it, but this will be an easy patch."

"I checked the rudder cables, and they are good. Ksenia will do an inspection when she gets here. As soon as we finish the fuselage patch we are done." Larissa said rubbing her cold hands together. "You know, I used to work on the Metrostroy. I even got to go underground and work."

"I thought women were not allowed down there," Rimma said working on the fuselage.

"They finally relented and let us down there to work," Larissa shrugged. "It was hard work and very scary at times. My older brothers got me the job, because they used to work on the underground railway system. They felt it was a very advanced idea for our Motherland." Larissa bowed her head for a moment and turned her face away from Rimma.

Rimma dropped her wrench, as she bent down to pick it up, she saw tears forming in Larissa's eyes. "Comrade, what is wrong? Tell me."

Larissa quickly composed herself, wiping her eyes with the cuff of her sleeve, "My three older brothers were killed during the first couple of months. I joined to try to stop this war before my younger brother is killed."

"My whole family was murdered by the Hitlerites, except my older sister Marina. When they attacked our village, we were both working on building an aerodrome that was far away from our village."

"Where is Marina now?"

"She is a sniper in the Red Army. Me, I loved working on planes. After I was through for the day working on the aerodrome some of the mechanics taught me how to work on the planes that were brought in."

"Why are you not a pilot?" Larissa asked.

"I like keeping my feet on the ground," Rimma laughed. "I have no desire to fly these things."

"That makes two of us," Larissa laughed.

A few moments later, Rimma stood back and looked at the patched-up plane. "There that is done. It is the best we can do," Rimma looked down the runway toward the mess hall. "Good thing we are done because here they come."

* * *

Darkness shrouded the camp as an evening mist slowly crept over the frozen airfield. Several small figures walked briskly in the cold air toward their battered and bullet-ridden airplanes, which loomed eerily against the heavy glow of the moon in the night sky.

"Are you ever afraid?" Lieutenant Natalya Mykolina asked. Her small gray eyes looked straight ahead as she walked toward her fragile Biplane.

Vera shrugged slightly. "Yes. I think we are all afraid we will not return. But is it not more frightening to have the Hitlerites win this war? It is an honor to die for our Motherland, although, like you, I would rather live for our Motherland. There will be peace and prosperity throughout our great country once we stop them."

"Yes, I understand all of that," Natalya nodded. "I was just feeling guilty because I become very frightened and when I land for refueling sometimes, I cannot stop my legs and body from shaking. I never want to show that fear to my navigator."

Vera stopped her and looked down at the thin, young girl. Her voice softened a little as she spoke, "I am sure your navigator is as frightened as you are. Sometimes Ksenia and I have bad fits after a sortie. And, then there are some sorties when we are not shaking so much or not at all. So, do not worry about that. For what we do, I think it is very normal."

"I guess you are right," Natalya sighed.

"It is what we must do. Life is not good so much now." She paused and then continued, "But it would be far worse under their control." Vera reached over and touched Natalya's arm. "You will be fine." She added. "We will all be fine. It is for our Motherland." Vera turned and headed toward her plane.

"I sure wish they would give us fighter planes to protect us." Natalya wiped her running nose with the cuff of her sleeve as she sped up to keep pace with her fast-moving Senior Lieutenant.

"They are needed to fight the fighter planes and bombers that the fascists are throwing at us." She said as they approached their respective planes.

Vera stood in front of her plane, took a deep breath, climbed onto the wing, and into her cockpit. She looked down and saw Ksenia, Rimma and Larissa staring up at her. "Come on," she motioned for Ksenia. "Time to drop our gifts to the Hitlerites. Payback time."

Ksenia nodded and straightened her shoulders, "Yeh, payback time."

Chapter 4

The next evening Vera and Ksenia made their way to their plane for their first sortie "That was a rough night last night." Ksenia said, as she checked out their plane as usual.

"In many more ways than one," Vera shook her head. "Horrible night. Not much sleep."

"Yeah, me too," Ksenia said slapping the side of the plane.

"Have you checked the bombs and made sure they are secured properly." Vera called out to two figures standing on the wings of the plane. She visually scanned the Biplane she was about to pilot and mumbled quietly to herself. "Death traps."

"What do you think? Of course, Comrade Sr. Lt. Zhlova." Rimma said greatly annoyed, as she and Larissa jumped off the wing. "These old planes are great training planes, but that is all they are good for."

"Oh, they are good for something. They are giving the fascists a lot of sleepless nights," Vera said.

"That is right. And, we will be here to keep it flight-ready," Larissa said nudging Rimma.

Rimma crossed her arms over her large bosom. The leather cap pulled snuggly around her head made her look older than her twenty years. "We do what we can. Although, I am a great mechanic, not sure about Larissa here," she said kiddingly. "She is a baby at eighteen."

Vera smiled, "I have the best mechanics on the field no matter what age. There is no question about that. Well," she reached out and stroked one of the wings of her plane, "it is all they had to give us. If we did not fly these planes, we would not be able to fly at all. These planes work for what we have to do."

"See," Rimma nudged Larissa, who just nodded.

"Hey," a deep, female voice called out from around the plane. Nice work patching up the holes caused by flak from last night."

"There was so much damage we had to wait until the sun came up to see all the problems," Rimma had her hands on her hips and looking proudly at how much they had gotten done during the day.

"Problems? You almost did not have a plane to fly today. I think we had about an hour's sleep to fix all the things that got shot up."

"As long as it can fly, and we can drop our payloads," Vera climbed into her cockpit. "We are good to fly."

"We will see you on your return," Rimma yelled, and softly she whispered, "Come back in one piece."

* * *

The Germans were prepared for them on each run; their plane was taking a bad beating. They landed after their sixth sortie, shaken up quite a bit, but alive. "You have your work cut out for you tonight," Vera quipped.

"We are seeing a lot more activity from them," Ksenia jumped to the ground.

"Come on," Vera grabbed Ksenia's arm, and they hurried to the mess hall.

A short while later Ksenia walked around the plane and spotted Vera. "Where have you been? Time to get going." Ksenia moved to the wing of their plane and smiled a big, toothy grin at her pilot. Her large, brown eyes had dark circles beneath them and her once creamy complexion was now ruddy-looking and drawn.

"You look like hell in this light, Ksenia" Vera said looking at her short, skinny navigator.

Ksenia nodded as her hair blew around her face. "At this point, I would look like hell in any light. There's a ringing in my ears. Unable to shake it like I did before. Kept me up all night."

"Yeah," Vera shrugged, "I get that too sometimes. Annoying consequence of flying for the Motherland."

"Wait? We went to the mess hall together, and then you disappeared. Where did you go?" Ksenia asked.

Vera shrugged as she adjusted her leather cap on, "A female problem."

"Okay, enough said," Ksenia looked at her plane and then at the mechanics. "I am assuming our plane is ready to fly."

"It is the best we can do," several dark strands of hair had escaped from Larissa's leather cap and blew around her face. Her gray eyes narrowed slightly. "Try not to get any more holes in this plane if you can, or you will be flying a plane with just a throttle stick and a pillow."

"What do you think?" Ksenia retorted to the mechanic. "Do you think that we fly around until we feel we have enough bullet holes in our plane?"

"So that is what you do up there," Larissa pretended to be serious. "I never knew."

"Well, now you do," Ksenia tried to hide a smile. "We do it because if there were no holes in the plane you would have no work. Working out in this weather is so much fun for you, is it not?"

"Yeah, about as much fun as having a picnic on top of an ant hill," Larissa laughed showing the deep dimples in her cheeks.

"In all seriousness, you take very good care of our plane. We have the best mechanics on the field," Ksenia nodded toward Rimma and Larissa.

Vera looked down with alarm at the face and hands of the two mechanics. "You two had better take care of your face and hands. They look froot bitten. You must go and get warm quickly."

"They have not given us indoor cover to repair these planes," Rimma said. "So, we do what we must."

"We will go back to our quarters and get warmed again," Larissa said. "You tell us to get warm, but you will also be very cold up there. It is bitter cold, and you have to fly in this open plane with no heat." She shook her head slowly.

"We do what we must, like Comrade Rimma said," Vera pulled her leather helmet over her woolen cap, tucked in her silk scarf at the neck of her jacket and eased herself onto the wing.

Rimma waited until Vera and Ksenia had climbed into their cockpits and went to the front of the plane winding the propeller to start the engine.

Quickly, Rimma gave the signal to go. Vera taxied down the field and lifted off into the dark, cold, cloudless sky. She looked behind her and saw that some of the other planes were now joining them.

"If Rimma thought it was cold on the ground she should be up here now," Vera yelled back to Ksenia. The arctic cold wind caused their goggles and windshields to fog up constantly as they flew in single formation toward their target.

Vera saw the lead plane waggle and knew the drop zone was just ahead. The steady drone of the planes died out one by one as they cut their engines. They approached the German camp gliding in low as usual. But something was different this time. Vera could feel it in her bones. Something bad was about to happen.

Suddenly, a brilliant light hit Vera's eyes, blinding her momentarily. There were more search lights than she could ever remember and at different angles making it harder to weave in and out of the lights.

The now familiar rat-a-tat sound of the machine guns blasted through the air, joined by the ack-ack sound of the German anti-aircraft mortars that were being launched at them. Their plane was being jostled about from the percussion of the flak bursting all around them.

Vera signaled Ksenia to get ready to drop their payload. Ksenia pulled up her goggles and leaned over the side of the plane to get a better view of her target like she always did. She waited for a moment and then pulled the lever releasing the bombs.

Vera pulled the plane up sharply. With the bombs gone, the plane was lighter and could climb faster. She began to circle around and head back to base when bullets from a machine gun strafed their plane. Bullets ricocheted off the engine striking the sleeve of Vera's jacket. Then, Vera's worst nightmare came true. Ksenia was screaming in pain, and their plane was badly hit.

The plane lurched and sputtered. Vera struggled to fly their plane a safe distance from the barrage of bullets erupting from below. She poured every ounce of strength she had into trying to control the plane. Slowly, the plane began to descend.

Tree tops brushed against the belly of her plane. And then she heard the sickening sound of her landing wheels being ripped off from the belly of the plane.

The plane was becoming harder to control as it skimmed over the trees. Desperately, Vera looked for a place she could land, as Ksenia's screams filled her head. She had to get her back to their base, but at the low level they were flying, nothing looked familiar.

Vera struggled with the jerking, sputtering plane as it began to descend even lower. Off to her left, she saw a winding creek below. It might be just wide enough for her to land their plane, she thought hopefully. In what seemed like minutes to Vera, but was only seconds, she managed to guide the plane over the creek. She pushed forward on the throttle to ease the plane down on the icy, rocky surface below.

The plane smacked the ground hard. It jerked and bucked as its belly scraped the rough terrain. Vera's hands gripped the steering column trying to keep the plane from hitting one of the trees that lined the creek.

She saw an opening through the trees and tried to steer her plane toward it. Finally, it came to a stop inches away from striking a tree. Vera climbed out onto the wing and reached for Ksenia. She stopped horrified at her still body. "No! No!" Vera screamed.

Ksenia turned her head slowly, "It is my leg. Help me get out," she spoke so softly Vera almost didn't hear her.

"Yes, yes," Vera was elated that her navigator, and friend, was still alive, even though by the looks of it just barely. "We have to get you help," she said struggling to get Ksenia out of her cockpit.

"Do you know where we are?" Ksenia asked weakly.

"No. I will check our map and see where we have landed."

Ksenia screamed when Vera tried to pull her out again. "You must save yourself," Ksenia said. "I saw a lot of movement on the road over there." She pointed a weak arm toward the direction where she had glimpsed them. "It may be the Germans."

"I am not leaving you for the Germans to get," Vera said emphatically.

"It could be our troops. You have to get to the road for help," Ksenia said weakly.

"Yes, yes. I saw the road. But I am not leaving you for the Germans." Vera stood looking down at her friend.

"I have my pistol. I will be all right. Vera, go. Go now," Ksenia pointed feebly toward the forest.

"Your wound looks very serious. Do not die on me Ksenia. I am your commanding officer, and I command that." She looked at the blood pumping from Ksenia's opened wound. "Before I do anything, I have to stop that bleeding."

Ksenia smiled weakly, "Do not worry about me. I will be fine. Just go."

"If I do not go for help you will surely die." Vera took off her silk scarf and looked around desperately for something to put pressure on Ksenia's wound, which was bleeding profusely. She took off her flimsy, leather helmet and the woolen cap she wore underneath it. She folded the cap and carefully placed it on Ksenia's wound. Ksenia grimaced but did not scream.

Vera took her silk scarf and began to wrap it over the cap. "It is not very clean, but I will not be long. At least the tourniquet will stop more blood loss." She paused for a moment and then added, "I hope."

As Vera tightened the silk scarf to add pressure to the wound, Ksenia's eyes rolled back in her head, and her body slumped down in her seat. Vera put her hand under Ksenia's nose to feel for any sign of breathing. She sighed with relief as she felt Ksenia's warm breath. "Please do not die my comrade, my dear comrade."

Quickly, Vera jumped off the wing and took out her map. She studied it for a moment. She pointed to a spot on the map. "Yes, this is where I saw the road. If I head toward it, I should reach one of our base camps in a couple of hours or less." She looked up at Ksenia's cockpit, "I will run all the way. I will get help." Stuffing the map back in her pocket Vera pressed through the trees in search of the road she had caught a glimpse of as their plane went down.

It was a long trek through the woods when Vera heard the rumbling of motor vehicles off in a distance. "A road," she exclaimed. Exhausted and out of breath, Vera found the strength to run as fast as she could to the road. Finally, she spotted the road, and stopped. She headed for a large clump of bushes that were close, but not too close to the road in case it was the Germans.

Vera waited until she recognized the Red Army decal on one of the trucks and rushed out from the bushes. She ran directly in the path of the lead jeep, waving her arms for it to stop.

Startled, one of the soldiers in the jeep raised his machine gun to fire at her. "Wait," an Army Sergeant yelled to his driver at the sight of Vera frantically waving the convoy of trucks down. He raised his arm signaling the trucks behind him to halt. "What is the matter with you? You nearly got yourself shot." He yelled at her.

"I am Senior Lieutenant Vera Zhkov, a pilot of the 588th regiment of the Red Army, and my navigator is wounded. I need help." She looked urgently into the sergeant's eyes.

"Sorry, we have Germans chasing us, and they are close behind. We had to evacuate our base." He shook his head and motioned with his hand for her to get away from the front of his jeep.

"I said I need help. I will not move. You will have to run me over or drag me off this road." Her eyes bore into his.

"I can do both," the Sergeant snapped at her.

A man in a camouflage suit walked up to the jeep. He looked intently at the young woman blocking their retreat. "What is the problem here?" He asked angrily.

Vera quickly recognized the insignia of a colonel on his shoulder patch and saluted.

"This crazy woman says she is a pilot, and her plane was shot down." The sergeant in the jeep laughed and gestured toward Vera.

"So, get in one of the trucks, and we will get you to the next base. You will be able to return to your unit then." The colonel looked perplexed. "This does not seem like a difficult problem sergeant."

Vera quickly spoke up. "Comrade Colonel, my navigator is badly injured, and I cannot get her out of the cockpit by myself. I need help." She looked at the tall, imposing colonel standing before her as she tried to fight back her frustration.

"Where is your plane?"

"About two miles that way," she pointed in the direction she had just come from.

"Get me a map sergeant," he ordered.

"I have one here, Comrade Colonel." She pulled the map from her pocket and spread it out over the back of the jeep, pointing to where her plane was.

The colonel studied the map for a moment and nodded. He showed her where he was going to be setting up base. "We should be there in about an hour. I can send this jeep," he pointed to the sergeant's jeep. "And I can spare two men to go back with you to get your navigator. This vehicle should be able to handle any terrain thrown at it."

The sergeant made a grumbling sound of disgust as he listened to the colonel.

The colonel looked down at the sergeant sitting in the jeep, "You will go with her and find her navigator and bring the wounded navigator back to our new base. That is an order. I will send a medic with you." It only took a moment for a medic to make his way to the colonel. He was quickly shown on the map which way they were to go, and where the new base was going to be set up.

"Thank you, Comrade Colonel," Vera quickly jumped into the back seat of the jeep.

"Move out," the sergeant yelled to the medic who climbed into the driver side. The medic turned the jeep into the grassy berm and raced through the trees.

The medic drove as fast as he could. He managed to avoid any major debris or holes in the ground as they bumped and jarred their way through the trees. No one spoke until they spotted the plane against a tree. "There! There it is!" Vera yelled, although it wasn't necessary as the two men spotted the plane at the same time.

"We are coming," Vera yelled. "I have found help, Ksenia. Help is coming!" She hoped Ksenia was still alive, and that they were not too late.

The medic pulled the jeep up to the wing of the plane, and all three occupants leapt from the jeep and climbed onto the wing of the plane. The medic quickly checked Ksenia's pulse. "She has lost a lot of blood, and her pulse is very weak. I fear we may not be able to save her."

"She is going to die," the sergeant grumbled. "I put my life in jeopardy for someone who is going to die anyway and for a stupid woman on top of everything."

Vera recoiled in disbelief and rage at the sergeant. She reached behind her and unsnapped the holster carrying her gun. She wanted to shoot the sergeant where he stood, and she did not care about the circumstances.

The medic heard the unsnapping of the holster and quickly placed his arm on Vera's shoulder. "Trust me I would do what you are thinking, too." Then a small smile crept across his face, "But it will take two men to get her out of there."

Vera never looked at the medic; she glared intently at the sergeant.

"What are you two thinking?" the sergeant asked gruffly.

"That in order to save this navigator, we have to get her out of the cockpit and into the jeep," the medic looked over at the sergeant who was still grumbling. "Or do you want to wait for the German's recon unit to find us?"

Ksenia did not wake up as they pulled her from the cockpit. The two men got her to the jeep and put her in the back seat. The sergeant got into the driver's seat and started up the engine. He put the gear into drive and began revving the engine. "Come on. Get moving!" he hollered.

"You ride up front with the sergeant. I will try to clean and treat the wound the best I can." The medic said to Vera, who was standing next to the jeep looking down at her wounded friend.

Just then a bullet whizzed by the Vera's head missing her by inches.

The sergeant hit the gas pedal and started driving away from the advancing German patrol. Vera dove toward the door of the jeep hanging half on and half out. The medic reached over and grabbed Vera's jacket, and with all his strength managed to pull her safely inside the truck. "What the hell were you going to do? Leave her there for the Germans to get?" The medic yelled angrily to the sergeant.

"She is not my responsibility," he snapped. "The colonel ordered me to pick up the wounded navigator. I did. And those Germans who were firing at us were on foot, and they have radios to give our location to the Germans. I am not getting killed for two useless, excuse me if I start laughing, women soldiers."

Bullets zinged and zipped around them. Vera and the medic bent over so their bodies were not exposed. The sergeant ducked down in his seat keeping his head just high enough to see where he was driving. He zigged and zagged the jeep through the trees causing most of the bullets to hit the tree trunks instead of the jeep. Soon the whiz and zing of the bullets stopped. Luckily, no one was shot and the jeep, although riddled with a few bullets, did not appear to have any real damage to it.

After everyone confirmed they had suffered no injuries, the medic's attention was now diverted to Ksenia. "I will do what I can to save her." He took off the tourniquet to see what damage had been done. "I will put medication to keep from an infection, but I have to leave this tourniquet to stop the bleeding. You did a very good job."

The sergeant mimicked the medic, "You did a very good job." He glanced back at the Medic and yelled angrily. "She nearly got me killed.

You call that a good job. She is a pretend pilot. A useless commodity to the Soviet people. I will bet she accidentally strayed into an air battle with real pilots fighting. She has no idea what danger really is."

"You really are an imbecile, Comrade Sergeant. So, therefore, I take no notice of the incompetency or illiteracy of a Neanderthal."

"What did she say? What did she call me, Medic?" He glared into the rearview mirror at the Medic.

"Sorry, I was not paying any attention. I am too busy trying to save this brave and honored woman's useless life." The Medic chuckled and continued to examine Ksenia's wound. "I am amazed. I cannot believe you fly those frail planes. There is no metal on your plane. Material and wood? I do not understand it at all. And you are the pilot of that death trap?" He asked Vera as he began to maneuver Ksenia's body in a position that would enable him to work on her wounds.

"Yes, and Ksenia is my navigator," she turned around and faced the medic. She was amazed by how gently the medic moved Ksenia's body so he could get to her wounds. She was so preoccupied with Ksenia; she had not really looked at the handsome medic.

"Pilot, what is your name?" Slowly, he moved so that he could rest Ksenia's head on the seat of the jeep.

"I am Senior Lieutenant Vera Zhkov. Vera to my friends. Please call me Vera." She kept looking from the face of the medic to Ksenia. "She is going to be alright. Is she not Comrade? I am sorry I did not get your name."

"Senior Medical Officer Yuri Dreklin, at your service. My friends call me Yuri," he gave a quick smile. "I brought my medic's bag, and I will need some things from it. It is on the floor by your leg. Can you help give me what I will need from the bag?"

"Yes, of course," Vera leaned forward and grabbed the medic's bag. "We were trained in first aid as well."

"Oh, I am so impressed that Vera knows how to fly a plane and even knows how to be a medic," The sergeant said sarcastically. "But does Vera know how to keep the Germans from shooting at us?" He snapped viciously.

"It is Sr. Lieutenant Zhkov to you," she said nonchalantly to the sergeant.

"I can stop this jeep right now and have you get out," he snarled looking over at her with anger raging across his face.

"If you stop this vehicle, I will shoot you before the engine shuts off." Her eyes narrowed as she reached behind to get her gun.

"I have a gun too, little girl," he said contemptuously.

"Me, too," the medic said somewhat happily. "So, if you stop, and she does not shoot you; I will."

The sergeant made a growling sound and continued speeding through the forest. Vera was sure that he purposely hit every bump, fallen log, and holes in the ground just to make sure treating Ksenia's wound would be more difficult and uncomfortable for them. She was grateful that Ksenia was unconscious or the trip for her would have been unbearable.

An hour later, they found the new base being set up. The sergeant pulled up to a small cottage and slammed on the brakes of the jeep. Vera was hurled into the windshield, and the medic and Ksenia were thrown into the back of the front seats.

The sergeant, who had braced himself for the sudden brake, laughed. "Well I got your navigator here." He opened the door and got out slamming the door behind him. He was walking away when Vera jumped over the closed door and ran after the sergeant. She reached him and got in front of him.

"What do you want, Senior Lieutenant Bitch?" he growled.

"Look," Vera pointed off to the right and the sergeant looked, but before he turned back to say something to her, she hit him in the stomach with all her strength.

The unexpected blow to his body caused the sergeant to double up.

While he was bent over for that fraction of a second, Vera pulled back her arm and slammed her elbow into his cheek.

He fell to the ground in shock. He got up slowly his eyes on fire with hatred and his body tensed to attack her, but he stopped with an intake of air.

Vera stood there with her pistol drawn and aimed at him. "Stay where you are," she yelled. "I will put a bullet in your fat head before you take one step. Some other things you do not know about us women pilots, we can shoot a gun and hit our targets, just as good as a man."

The medic was already by Vera's side and staring at the sergeant who was carefully standing up and keeping a watchful eye on the gun in Vera's hand.

"What is going on over there?" The colonel yelled standing beside one of the trucks being unloaded a few cottages away.

"She pulled a gun on me," the sergeant yelled, pointing at the still raised gun in Vera's hands.

"What?" The colonel began to walk toward Vera and the sergeant. He looked at the gun in Vera's hand, and back at the sergeant. "What happened?"

"I believe the sergeant is not a true Citizen of the State. He is an embarrassment to our Unit and the Red Army," the medic said. He reached over and lowered the gun in Vera's hand. "Put it away," he said gently and walked toward the approaching colonel.

"I want reports from all of you, now!" The colonel glared at both the sergeant and Vera.

Slowly, Vera lowered her gun and put it back into its holster. No sooner had she holstered her gun when the sergeant charged and knocked her to the ground. An ugly grin crossed his face as he strad-dled her and then his fist slammed into her jaw. Just as he was about to strike again Yuri raced back and kicked him hard in the face sending him off her sprawling in the dirt.

"Enough," yelled the colonel. "Have the sergeant put in restraints until I clear this matter up," he yelled to several soldiers who had come over to see what the ruckus was about.

"Colonel, please, my navigator." Vera could hardly speak as she held her sore jaw.

"I will take care of it," Yuri said, and as he helped Vera off the ground, he began barking orders to several men standing around, "Take the wounded officer in the jeep to the hospital tent immediately." He looked at Vera. "I think you will need some looking after as well." He gently ushered her into the hospital tent.

"Comrade," he said to a woman standing near a wounded patient. "Have Comrade Zoffko look after that navigator," he pointed to Ksenia, who was just being brought in. "And then look after this pilot. I have to go and see the colonel, and I will be back as quickly as I can." He walked from the tent. It was a long while before he returned.

Vera sat holding a cold, wet cloth against her injured jaw. She looked up as Yuri walked in. The first thing he did was check on Ksenia, and then he walked over to Vera.

"She will be out of service for a while. Comrade Zoffko, who is a very competent doctor, believed it was your tourniquet that saved her life," he smiled. He reached over and tilted her head so that he could see her chin better in the light. "Well, you will have a very nasty bruise on that jaw for a while."

"I want to thank you for everything you have done," Vera's words were stilted because of the pain from her jaw. "You are a wonderful medic."

"Actually, I am a doctor, too" he said pulling up a chair and sitting next to her. "I had an interesting conversation with the colonel about your 'friend' the sergeant," he said sarcastically. "He is being sent to the front lines. He is lucky that he is not being put in front of a firing squad for attacking a ranking officer. Firing squad or the front lines? Those were the only two choices the colonel gave him."

"I know I will have to answer for my drawing a weapon on a fellow officer," she dropped her head.

"After I gave my report the colonel said the only problem, that he could see, is that you did not shoot him. He said he would have," Yuri reached over and patted Vera's hand. "I think you need some rest for now. I will keep a watchful eye on your friend."

"I cannot rest. I have to get back to my base." Vera began to stand up and felt a wave of nausea sweep over her. She fell back onto the chair.

"There is no way for you to get back to your base tonight. However, there is a plane due either tonight or tomorrow morning with medical supplies. You can fly back with them in the morning. But for now, you must rest." He stood up and reached his hand down to Vera. "Come I will take you to the women's quarters where you can sleep for the night."

Vera studied the doctor as he led her to a camouflaged tent surrounded by a mass of trees. He was very nice looking and tall. He had deep green eyes, and his short, blond hair had a reddish cast to it. He was very thin and not muscular at all. Vera kept up with his fast pace. She wanted to know more about this kind and gentle man. "Where is your family staying? I hope they are in a safe city right now," she said sincerely.

"My wife was killed about a year ago shortly after the war broke out. The Germans bombed our city and one of the bombs struck our home. I was at the hospital at the time." He looked over at Vera, and his voice seemed to crack just slightly. He cleared his throat, "What about your family? Husband and children?"

"I have neither," she said shyly. "I have no fiancé or boyfriend to worry about me either."

"It seems we have a lot in common," he smiled warmly. "I have no fiancé or boyfriend either."

A small laughed escaped Vera's lips.

"It would please me very much if you would let me write to you." He said.

"I would like that very much as well," Vera smiled warmly.

He stopped at the entrance to the women's quarters. "It has been a pleasure meeting you, and I sincerely mean that."

"I believe the pleasure was mine," said Vera.

They stood looking at each other for a while not knowing what to do next. Their uncomfortable position ended when a woman pulled back the flap of the tent and startled them.

"Oh, Comrade Corporal, I would greatly appreciate your helping this pilot find a place to sleep for the night," Yuri bowed slightly to the woman.

"Yes, Comrade Doctor, I will have her sleep on my bed as I have the night shift tonight," she turned and opened the flap again.

"Good night then Comrade Sr. Lieutenant," he bowed deeply to Vera, turned and walked away.

Vera followed the woman into the tent where plank boards were lined up in neat little rows with a blanket thrown on top of them. After the woman showed her where everything was, and Vera was resting on the bed, her thoughts went to Yuri. There was a strange tugging at her heart at just the thought of his name. Shortly, even the thoughts of Yuri faded as Vera lapsed into a deep, much-needed rest.

Chapter 5

The freezing, cold winds blew under the tent and through its canvas walls chilling her to the core. Vera tried to be useful by helping at the hospital tent. She was not a trained nurse but followed Yuri's gentle instructions assisting him wherever she was needed.

Vera hunted through the forest, digging through the snow for wood to keep the fire in the large oil containers burning in the hospital. It was the only heat they had against the constant freezing winds.

When she could, she sat by Ksenia's cot waiting for her to regain consciousness. She was relieved when finally, Ksenia opened her eyes.

"Did we make it?" Ksenia asked feebly.

"Yes. Yes, we did," Vera took her hand and held it firmly in hers.

"Where are we?"

"We are at a hospital base camp," Vera looked over at Yuri, who was standing next to Ksenia's bed. "You are in the best hands you could ever hope to be. This is comrade Senior Medical Officer Yuri Dreklin. We owe our lives to him."

"I see," Ksenia smiled. "Thank you Comrade Dreklin. How badly have I been damaged?"

Yuri gave a short laugh, "Damaged? I would say the damage, although painful for now, will heal perfectly. You will be like new in no time."

"That is what I wanted to hear," Ksenia smiled. "How long have I been here? We have to get back up in the air."

"You are in no condition to fly right now," Yuri said. "It will take you some time before you are completely healed."

"Besides that fact, there is a major storm brewing outside. Not even I could get back to base." Vera gently placed Ksenia's hand under the covers. "Stay warm and rest for now, comrade." She adjusted the covers up around Ksenia's neck and watched as she drifted off to sleep.

As the winter storm raged for two days, Yuri and Vera grabbed every little moment they had to be together. They talked of their lives before the war and their plans for after the war. Vera found herself falling in love with this kind and gentle man. She tried to fight the feeling, but she knew it was hopeless: She fell deeply in love with him.

On the third morning, Vera was startled awake by a loud explosion followed by the rumble of trucks and shouts from outside her tent. The flap to the tent flew open and several women rushed in and began grabbing clothing and other items from inside the tent.

The corporal, whose cot she shared, ran to Vera. "We are moving out," she said excitedly. "The Germans are getting close. We have to get moving, now."

"You are moving the base camp?" Vera was still disoriented.

Suddenly, another loud booming sound slammed through the air shaking the ground beneath her.

"What was that?" Vera asked in alarm.

"German artillery. We thought we had managed to get far enough away from enemy lines, but the Germans broke through our defenses this morning and are headed this way. You must get out of my way," she said briskly.

"Yes. Yes, of course," Vera said now fully awake. She had fallen asleep in her clothes and shoes, so it made it easy for her to get off the plank board quickly. The women were tearing down the bed boards and throwing them at the entrance to the tent. Soldiers outside the tent were grabbing everything and putting it into a truck sitting by the entrance.

Vera hurried out of the tent and almost ran into Yuri as he was coming toward her.

"Comrade Sr. Lt. Zhkov." He spoke to her formally in front of every-one as he took Vera by the arm and led her away. He found a secluded spot a short distance among a sparsely treed area. "I wanted to say good-bye before we left. Your navigator, Comrade Ksenia, was taken by truck to a hospital along with the other wounded this morning. She was in good form and told you not to worry she would be back for duty as soon as her wound heals properly."

More German artillery smashed through the air, only nearer now.

"Will the wounded be safe with the Germans coming up from be-hind us?"

"Yes, they have a great head start and will be deep within Soviet held territories and safe. I was busy getting them out of here as fast as I could because it has been said that the fascists kill any wounded they find left behind."

"But what of you? Why are you not with them?" Worry etched across Vera's face.

"I was busy loading up medical supplies and equipment. Do not worry. I am taking the next truck out of here. It leaves in just minutes. That is why I rushed over here to say good-bye." He took her hands in his. "My dear, brave Vera," he dropped his head down and looked at their hands. When he looked up, there were tears forming in his eyes, "I do not mean this to sound brazen, but I have come to care for you a great deal."

"Come on Medic," a soldier standing by a truck yelled.

"I care for you as well," Vera said with tears running down her face. She didn't wait for anything else to be said; instead, she threw her arms around him, and kissed him soundly on the lips.

Yuri returned her kiss, held her tightly one last time, and hurried to the waiting truck. "I will write to you as soon as I can," he yelled. He climbed in back of the truck and waved to Vera as his truck pulled away.

She could barely see his truck leaving, because the air was filled with smoke from the artillery guns firing all around them.

Vera hurried to the base commander's tent. He was busy stuffing the last of his papers into a large, wooden box.

"What can I do to help?" She asked him.

"You can bomb the hell out of them for us," he said never lifting his head as he kept stuffing the box.

"I can do that for you, but I have to get back to my base first." She stepped back as a soldier rushed into the tent and grabbed a box crammed to the brim sitting by the commander's feet.

"A plane just landed a few moments ago. She seemed very excited that you, and your navigator, were safe. She said she will take you back to your base," he said.

"I did not hear it land?" Vera said in shock.

"With all the noise from the German artillery, it is no wonder," he said studying a piece of paper for a moment and then shoving it into a box.

"I suggest you find the pilot and get out of here now," he stopped and looked at her for the first time. "The Germans are very close, but the pilot is ready to fly out now."

"Where is the pilot?" Vera's spirits were lifted at the thought of returning to her base.

"I am here," a soft female voice from behind Vera said. "Hello Comrade Vera."

Vera turned seeing her friend, Sr. Lt. Elena Petrovka. "Comrade Elena, I am glad it is you I will be flying with."

"If you women will excuse me; I have to catch my jeep and get out of here." The colonel passed them carrying his box of papers.

"Yes, Comrade Colonel," they replied at the same time.

Elena and Vera hurried to the open field where her plane had landed. "We saw you shot down and hoped you had made it out safely. I started to come back for you, but a couple of Messers came out of nowhere, and I had to hide in the clouds until I felt they were gone. By then my fuel was too low."

"Did everyone get back safely?" Vera's voice filled with hope.

"Yes. Comrades, Stana and Olga, were wounded, but not too badly."

"How did you land with all the German guns firing around here?"

"I had no choice. You know what that is like," she chuckled as they hurried to her plane. "I was told I had urgent papers to deliver to the colonel at this base. So, here I am."

Another loud boom and the earth shook under their feet. "How close are they?

"They are situated further to the east. My plane is parked way west of them."

"Mercy, they sound close," Vera cringed as another artillery shell exploded. "I am so glad you found out I was here."

Elena chuckled for a moment. "That colonel is not very talkative. I was just getting ready to leave, when he said that another pilot had been shot down along with her navigator a couple of days ago, and the pilot was still at the base. I immediately asked where you were. He said the navigator had been badly wounded and taken to a city where there is good treatment for her. However, the pilot is still here. He pointed in your direction."

"That is a lucky day for me," Vera smiled.

"Well, I saw a handsome man taking you by the arm. I wanted to give you your privacy, so I waited until I saw him get in the truck."

Vera glanced over at Elena and smiled. It never stopped to amaze her how lovely Elena was, even with the smoke and soot on her face. The sky was clear blue making Elena's blue eyes appear bluer, and her curly, blond hair framed her face accenting her delicate features.

"I am glad Ksenia will be taken care of properly," Elena said stepping gingerly over a small, fallen tree. "It is good to have you back again, Vera."

"Thank you, Elena." Vera abruptly changed the subject. "So, how many hearts have you broken lately?" she asked with a smile.

"I have stopped counting," Elena looked up at Vera and they both started to laugh.

"I can assume you flew sorties all night," Vera said as they hurried toward their plane.

"Of course, did you know that we women do not need sleep to function," Elena laughed. "Not only that, when that blizzard hit a couple of days ago, I was forced to land in a field. I had no food for two days, and nearly froze to death. Although, I had all the snow I could eat. Luckily, I got the plane started when the storm ended, and I could fly out of there to get here just in time for a German blitz."

"So, you have flown from one storm into another," Vera said shaking her head.

"Just another delightful day in the army," Elena smiled wickedly as they reached her plane.

Vera flipped the propeller, and the engine started up. She hurried to the side of the plane and climbed into the navigator's seat.

Their plane traveled a short distance down a bumpy, snow covered field until it finally became airborne. Vera felt comfortable with Elena's flying, because she was probably the best pilot in the entire division. Only too soon Vera's opinion of Elena's prowess as a pilot became completely verified.

Out of nowhere, two German Messerschmitts appeared from out of a bank of clouds.

"Messers," Elena screamed back to Vera. "Hold on."

Elena pushed the throttle to full power, as Vera saw the flashes of the Messerschmitts guns. The bullets zinged by their weaponless plane, just missing them both.

The enemy fighters were almost on them when Elena broke a hard right, and the Messerschmitts flew past them. They were so close Vera could see the surprised look on one of the German pilot's face.

Their fragile plane swayed in the enemy's slipstream as Elena struggled to maintain control of their plane.

The German planes had to make a wide turn to circle back, which gave Elena a chance to dive toward the cover of the trees below. Now they were flying at tree-top level when the German fighter planes came in for another strike. Elena pulled on the throttle and broke into a hard left. Bullets from the German fighters strafed the wing of the plane, ripping more holes in the canvas.

The Messerschmitts made another large arc to return and finish off the little Biplane.

A river, frozen over, gave Elena a wide berth to fly her plane beneath the trees without it being ripped apart by the barren branches. The river opened into a large area giving Elena the opportunity to veer sharply to the right.

One of the German pilots spotted her change, and intent on the kill, pulled his plane sharply to the right, causing the other plane to graze him. Suddenly, the two enemy fighters were struggling to get control of their planes, and to both women's delight and relief, the two Messerschmitts crashed into a copse of trees below.

The rest of their trip back to base was uneventful. When they landed Vera got out on the wing of their badly shot up plane. "That was great flying up there," she said to Elena. "You should transfer to the fighter division."

"Funny you should say that." Elena flashed her winning smile. "I have been assigned to a fighter unit. I leave today for training. This was my last run in this unit."

"Lucky for me, it was you I got to fly with today," Vera said with relief.

"I have seen you fly with great expertise. You would have done exactly what I did. You are an excellent pilot Vera," Elena said sincerely. "Do not ever doubt that."

Vera stopped and looked at the surrounding area. The terrain did not look familiar to her. "Where are we?"

"This is our new base," Elena gestured grandly at their surroundings. "This is where they moved our base about two days ago. You are not getting used to this yet?" Elena laughed. "This is the third time in two weeks."

The two women were quickly greeted by Elena's and Vera's ground crews. After the warm reception, the two women walked toward base headquarters.

Vera tugged at her dirty britches and squirmed. "I know this is not of any great importance, but I would love to get into women's underwear."

"Oh, yes, and how about boots that fit us so nicely," Elena said sarcastically. "There are more newspapers stuffed in my boots than feet."

"At one point, I was thinking of taking one of the silk parachute sails from one of our flares to make some women's underwear, but at another base, two women did just that and got into a lot of trouble for destroying government property." Vera shook her head. "At another base, four women were sentenced to fifteen days in prison for altering their uniforms."

"That is terrible," Elena's voice registered shock. "If they gave us women's uniforms, boots and underwear we wouldn't have to go to such extremes. Why has not the government provided us with proper equipment? I think it is poor planning on our government's part."

"You can say that to me but be careful. You could be shot for saying such things." Vera looked around them to make sure no one could hear them. "And just so you know; I absolutely agree with what you said. Although, I am surprised we did not get sent to prison when we altered our uniforms the first time."

"Probably because the last time they cut down my uniform, they had enough material to make another. Economics!" Elena laughed.

"I am going to miss you, Elena," Vera reached her arm around Elena's shoulders.

"I will miss you, too," Elena reached up and patted one of Vera's hands and slid her other hand around back of Vera's waist as they walked to the base headquarters. "I have come to love all the women in our unit as sisters."

"Absolutely," Vera said. "I hope we all will be friends for the rest of our lives."

Chapter 6

Several weeks later, Vera was given a dispatch to the fighter squadron stationed near the Russian front. She had to keep checking the map to make sure she was headed in the right direction. One wrong turn and she would be flying directly over enemy territory.

Vera was carefully plotting her flight route when she looked up and saw a Messerschmitt coming straight at her. She dropped the map and banked quickly to the right. The German fighter guns flashed as they poured bullets at her. She flipped her plane hard to the left, as another spray of bullets zinged by her, just missing her plane.

The Messerschmitt circled back and was coming in behind her. Fear struck Vera, because she knew it now had a direct line of fire on her plane. There were no trees below to try to hide among. She was caught out in the open with no way to avoid being struck down.

Suddenly, she saw movement above. Another fighter plane was speeding toward her. She let out a yelp. It was one of theirs; a Soviet Yakovlev fighter. The YAK-1 plane dove in fast and sent a row of bullets at the German fighter plane. The Messerschmitt swung up, forgetting about Vera and her little Biplane, and began attacking the fighter.

But the lone YAK-1 fighter pilot was not to be taken down. The Messerschmitt began chasing and firing at the Soviet plane as it banked left and right. The chasing enemy fighter could not get a clear shot at the YAK-1 as it constantly out maneuvered it. Then, the Soviet fighter plane went straight up into the sky and came up behind the surprised enemy pilot. Vera watched as the YAK-1's guns opened up with a fiery burst at the Messerschmitt, causing it to erupt into flames and explode, sending a burning mass to the ground.

Vera and the YAK-1 pilot landed at the base field. Vera waited until the pilot got out of the plane and was surprised to see that it was Elena.

"Hello Comrade," Elena smiled. "I am glad to see you."

"I can say I am doubly glad to see you," Vera smiled broadly. "It was lucky for me that you were patrolling the area."

"I was not patrolling," she said. "I finished my pilot training and was assigned to this base. I was en route to report to this base when I saw the Messer attacking one of our planes, I think shooting it down was a great way to report to my first day as a fighter pilot."

"You are a great pilot," Vera said to the diminutive woman walking beside her. "You were transferred here, and it was a good day for them and me. I have seen for myself what a great fighter pilot you are. However, I would expect nothing less from you."

"We are all fine pilots, are we not?" Elena's clear, sky-blue eyes looked up at Vera. "It is very different from dropping our payloads and then scurrying back to base, reloading, and going back up again every five minutes. And, I feel it is no less dangerous than flying a fighter plane, only now I can shoot back." Elena stopped and touched Vera's arm. "You know you are a very excellent pilot. Maybe they could transfer you here?"

"I am a very good pilot, but not in your caliber. You seem to have been born with this wonderful gift of flying. You do it so effortlessly."

"Oh, not so effortlessly. I had to work very hard. The speed of our duckling U2 is very slow compared to the fighter I must fly. I had to fly and shoot better than the men in our training, because I do not think they wanted to waste a fighter plane on a woman." Elena said.

"Do you still need a cushion in the YAK-1?" Vera asked. "I only know of one woman in our regiment that does not need one. However, she is almost six feet tall. I know I would have a hard time flying without mine."

"You should have seen the look on their faces when I brought my cushion to sit on. I could not reach anything, in fact; I could barely see through the cockpit window dome. Even my little cushion did not help much. But I figured out, if I sit on my cushion *and* my parachute, I am as tall as any of the men." Elena looked around them to see if anyone could hear them. Satisfied that no one was around, she continued. "I am going to tell you a little secret, some of the shorter male pilots need a cushion as well." She looked up at Vera and then the two women began to laugh.

"I can believe that," Vera said.

"Of course," Elena shrugged, "having them fit a box over the pedals, so I could reach them, was another thing that made them laugh about women flying planes."

"Once they witness your excellent flying skills, I do not think they will be laughing for long," Vera said earnestly.

"Anyway, why do they find it so hard to believe that women can handle flying fighters, or, any of our planes? I believe I had more problems with the men's view of women flying planes than studying to be a fighter pilot. Especially the higher-ranking officers."

"I know," Vera said. "Somehow, I know this sounds crazy, but I think that our superiors feel we women are expendable."

"Yes, I agree," Elena nodded.

"Well, if nothing else, I think you have proven without a doubt that women are as capable and dangerous as the men when we fight, are we not?" Vera smiled down at Elena.

"Oh, yes!" Elena nodded. "Oh yes, we are. Look at how many times we were sent out at night to bomb the Germans in all kinds of weather and in total darkness."

"That still has not changed," Vera said.

"I wish you luck and safe returns my friend." Elena began looking around the airfield. "Are you familiar with this base?"

"Yes," I just delivered a dispatch to the base commander," Vera said.

"You delivered a dispatch?" Elena asked in surprise. "I thought they had more recruits, and they were going to be handling those missions to relieve the night-bombers daytime duties."

Vera stopped and looked at Elena, "The other women's division suffered heavy casualties yesterday. Four pilots and four navigators were attacked and shot down. There were no survivors. Not one of them was over twenty years old." She paused and shook her head slowly. "So, we have been instructed to pick up their war efforts, until their replacements can be made."

"I am sorry to hear that," Elena said sincerely. "Very sorry to hear that, and very angry. I am here now and will have a great opportunity to avenge them. You can count on that. I want to get in the air as fast as possible, so if you can tell me where the flight command center is situated I will report to the Flight Commander."

Vera walked toward the base headquarters and stopped. "There," she said pointing to a large house across the field. "There is where you will find the Flight Commander and the rest of the pilots." She turned and pointed across the field to a smaller house. "Over there, far away from the men, are your women's quarters." She looked at Elena and shrugged. "A couple of days ago, I had to spend the night due to really bad weather. Best of luck to you, Comrade, I have to return to my base for more orders or hopefully a little sleep."

"I will head to the women's quarters and drop off my belongings first. Best of luck to you, Comrade Vera," Elena said pulling her flying jacket around her in a futile attempt to keep warmer.

Elena walked into her new quarters and thought they were slightly better than the dugouts she lived in while she was with the night bombers. It was a home that was partially bombed, but there was a roof over her head and a large, unlit fireplace in the middle of the room. Stacked neatly by the fireplace was kindling and firewood. There was no indoor plumbing, so she knew she would have to find where the toilet was located. After checking out the four cots lined up in two neat rows, she selected the cot nearest the fireplace.

Elena hurried to the base commander and checked in. Afterward, she was getting hungry and stopped a soldier and asked where the mess hall was located. He pointed to a large house and told her she had better hurry because the mess hour was just about through.

The flight in was cold, and she didn't feel any warmer on the ground as she hurried toward the regiments' mess hall. Everyone was busy talking and paid no attention to her as she stood last in the long line to get food.

A few minutes later, the door to the mess hall opened with a loud bang. "Sorry, the wind has picked up," a female voice yelled out.

Elena turned to see two women walk into the room. The much larger of the two women grabbed the door and pulled it shut. They walked to the mess line and stood directly behind her.

After a couple of minutes, Elena got her food, a bowl of cabbage soup, bread, and a cup of coffee when she heard one of the women behind her talking to her friend. Elena turned slightly and out of the corner of her eye; she saw it was the larger woman talking about her.

"That little thing needs bird food, not human food."

The other woman laughed, "I sure hope she is not flying a fighter."

"I do not think they make fighter planes in miniature," the burly woman spoke loudly.

Both women laughed as they got their food next. Then Elena turned around, and both women saw that she was a Senior Lieutenant. Elena looked at them both up and down for a moment and saw the startled look on their faces when they realized they were making fun of a higher-ranking officer.

"This little bird has a very mean peck," Elena said. She walked away and sat at a table by herself.

The two women sat on the other side of the mess hall, as far away from Elena as they could get.

After her meal, Elena headed to her barracks and noticed that a fire had been started and was burning warmly in the room. She was very cold and moved toward the fire that was now blazing brightly in the fireplace.

She shivered as the wind howled through the thick, heavy wooden door. She could feel a cold draft slipping through the thin strips of wood that were sparsely nailed over the broken windows.

Elena took off her gloves and warmed her hands by the fire. Soon she started to become warmer and took off her jacket and threw it on top of her cot.

The wooden door opened and the two women she had encountered in the mess hall came bursting through the door. "It sure is getting colder," the bigger woman said looking back at her friend and closing the door behind them. She did not see Elena standing there until she turned toward the fireplace. Both women stopped and stared at Elena for a moment.

"Comrade Senior Lieutenant we are sorry for being so discourteous in the mess hall earlier," the tall woman said in a very, deep voice.

"I am not offended by being called a bird," Elena smiled and turned to the two women. "I love flying and wish I could fly like a bird without a plane."

The two women visibly relaxed as Elena's smile assured them there were no hard feelings.

The smaller woman saluted Elena, "I am Corporal Aleksandra Kodovik. Best mechanic of the Red Army." Her short, reddish-blond hair curled slightly at the nape of her neck. Her angular face cracked into a big smile. She was not exceptionally pretty, but there was a freshness about her young face.

"Comrade Lieutenant Oxana Jurvoika, new pilot of the 45th Red Army fighter regiment." She walked over to the fireplace and rubbed her red hands together to try to get them warm. "You must have been at Engels the same time as me. Sorry, we did not meet at the training center, but I did not have time to get to know anyone. I was studying very hard. I wanted to be a fighter pilot. That was the most important thing to me." She spoke in a deep and loud voice. Then she paused for a moment and looked down at Elena. "Say you are kind of short to be flying those big fighters. I am not sure I want you as my wingman, that's for sure."

"I can hold my own against the best of them," Elena said defiantly looking her straight in the eye. "Comrade Senior Lieutenant Elena Petrovka. And, you do not have to worry about my being your wingman. I have already been assigned."

"It is just that," Oxana stopped and looked at Elena questioningly. "Did you say Senior Lieutenant Petrovka?"

"Yes," Elena replied stoically.

Oxana threw her head back and laughed heartily. "So, you are the one I was constantly trying to beat. I take back what I said. I want you as my wingman. I was constantly studying and practicing for hours and hours just to compete with you. And just for the record, so were the men."

"I only got a glimpse of you and the other female pilot from the training, because I too just wanted to study and be my best." Elena smiled at the tall, buxom woman.

"I kept asking, who is this Petrovka person, and one day one of the other pilots tried pointing you out to me. But you were moving very quickly, and before I could get a clear view of you, you disappeared into a mass of taller males."

"There was another woman pilot in our training group. I wonder if she passed," Elena said.

"Yes, she did. She is an excellent pilot as well. I met up with her just before they sent me out. Senior Lieutenant Sophie Cherkov was supposed to join us, but then her orders came, and she was assigned to another division. That is a shame. She is a spitfire. A lot of fun when we were not studying. We roomed together. Where were you?"

"I was billeted with a family near the airfield with another girl," Elena's toned changed and sadness crept into her voice. "She was killed during a practice run, and then they moved me to the training center."

"I heard about one of the women pilots crashing her plane," Oxana said. Her voice filled with anger, "They were worried about getting another plane to fill the one she destroyed. They did not seem to care that she was killed, just the loss of a plane. Every time I went to fly someone would warn me not to crash my plane. And there was always a male asking what are you women doing flying fighters for anyway? Women should be home in the kitchen," Oxana shook her head.

"What did you say to that?" Elena asked.

"Told him I cooked a pig once and it looked just like him," Oxana laughed.

"I got the same comments, even more so, because I am so short. They said things like 'you are so attractive' you should be home making babies." Elena shrugged. "Some of them were so brazened as to say that they would help me make a baby and show me how it was done."

"Pigs!" Oxana spat out.

"But I did not care what they said. I wanted to fly a fighter plane and kill Hitlerites and rid our country of them. I just want peace again."

Me, too," Oxana said. "Umm, just so you know; I am a great fighter pilot, too. Well, I am glad we cleared things up."

"This is going to be really different for me," Elena said.

"What is going to be different?" Aleksandra asked.

"I came from an all-female regiment," Elena shrugged. "This ought to be very interesting."

"Well, you still have a female mechanic," Aleksandra smiled. "I will not know which one of your planes I will be working on until I get my orders. But I will be honored to work on either one of yours."

Oxana put her arm around Aleksandra's shoulder, "She was the best in her class from what I hear from the other mechanics. We met on the flight over here."

Elena smiled and nodded, "We women will do just fine here. The men will have to step it up to best any of us."

Oxana laughed heartily, "Comrade Elena, I am glad to meet you. I think we are going to be life-long friends."

"I would like that," Elena said. They each walked to their plank bed near the fireplace. "Are these cots going to be long enough for you?" Elena exclaimed sizing up the bed and then Oxana.

"If not, I will put two together," Oxana replied half-jokingly. She took her duffel bag off her cot, threw it on the floor, and stretched out on the bed still in her jacket, cap and boots. "Yes, I do fit. But just barely."

Elena scratched her head and shook her hair out. "I would give anything to be able to wash this hair."

"Me, too," Oxana smiled and jumped up. "Come on," she said as she grabbed an empty bucket by the door.

"Where are we going?" Elena asked perplexed.

"To wash our hair," Oxana laughed and raced out the door.

"It's freezing out there. So, I will stay here and keep the fire going," Aleksandra yelled after them.

"We do not have enough water to wash our hair." Elena protested as she grabbed her flight jacket, gloves and hat, and quickly followed after Oxana.

"Hurry up," Oxana said running to their planes. The mechanics were not around as she opened the water intake that cooled off the engines. Steaming, hot water poured out of the intake and into the bucket. "Now we just put some snow in here, and we will have enough warm water to wash our hair," Oxana stood facing Elena with her chest pushed out. "Clever, no?"

"Clever, yes!" Elena laughed. "The mechanics have to drain all this water anyway because it would freeze up."

They both chuckled and raced back to their quarters.

After they had all finished washing their hair, and letting it dry in front of the fireplace, they fell into their beds with their clothes on.

Aleksandra was the first to fall asleep and was snoring gently.

Oxana pulled the woolen blanket up around her neck and looked over at Elena, who had done the same thing. "Say, did you meet our new flight commander yet? Commander Sr. Major Nikolai Belko? He flew in just before you landed. He cuts quite a figure. Very handsome man. He could put his boots under my cot any time."

"No, I did not meet him yet. I wonder how he will react when he realizes I am his new wingman," Elena put her arm behind her head and looked up at the cracked lines running through the ceiling.

"You two would make a great-looking couple." Oxana said and rolled over on her side and simply said. "Good night."

"Good night," Elena replied and fell asleep thinking about tomorrow's flight plans.

* * *

The next morning, after having her morning meal of bread, cheese and coffee, Elena entered the base flight command room. A tall, handsome man was standing before the men pointing to a map on a long table. One foot was on a chair seat, and his forearm rested on that leg.

A couple of small lanterns were used for lighting and placed directly on the table near the maps. Nearby was a kerosene heater emitting a warm glow.

The flight commander did not look up as he yelled to Elena, "Put your gear by the door." He returned to pointing out places on the map for the men sitting around the table.

Elena took off her gloves and then her over-sized flight jacket and placed it on a pile of coats thrown over a chair. She took off her leather pilot helmet, and woolen cap, and shook out her curly, now shoulder-length, blonde hair.

"You are late," the commander snapped. "You were..." He stopped abruptly as he looked up and saw the pilot. It was a woman. All the men turned to see what had interrupted the commander's admonishment of a fellow fighter pilot.

Elena turned to the commander; she could feel all the men staring at her. She moved out of the shadows toward the table, and as she neared the two lanterns, she could hear the intake of air from the men surrounding it. "Senior Lieutenant Petrovka reporting for assignment."

The commander's foot fell off the chair with a thud. The closer she got the men could see how beautiful she was, and everyone was silent for a moment. Finally, the commander mumbled "Commander Sr. Major Belko," and nodded for her to sit at the table. After an hour, the commander finished explaining the flight path and who was assigned to whom. Elena was to be his wingman. Their first flights would start tomorrow early in the morning.

Everyone filed out of the shelter and headed toward their quarters. Commander Belko reached over and touched Elena's arm. "Stay for a moment," he said quickly. "I was given notice that an honored pilot was going to join our group. They told me it was a pilot who excelled in training above all others and was being assigned to my command, and that I should be honored." He cleared his throat, "They seem to have forgotten to tell me that this excellent pilot was a woman."

"It is I who am honored to serve under your command," she nodded respectfully as she studied his handsome face. His dark-brown eyes seemed almost as black as his hair, and when he smiled, a large dimple appeared in his cheek. She handed him her papers. "Does it matter?"

"Does what matter?" He asked.

"That this excellent pilot is a woman," she said studying his face intently.

"No. No, it does not." He started to read the papers she handed him and looked up at her in surprise. "I cannot believe that you have accomplished as much as you have in so short a time, and being a..." he stopped.

"And being a woman," her eyes narrowed at him.

"Yes, because you are a woman. Not only are you a woman, but a beautiful woman."

"Beauty has nothing to do with my achievements," she bristled slightly. "Do they base your achievements on your handsome face?"

The commander threw back his head and laughed, "Of course not. It is just a shock to see such a tiny, beautiful woman take on the big, bad, ugly Hitlerites."

"I am ready to take on the big, bad, ugly Hitlerites."

"You were used to flying the U-2's," he stopped for a moment. "Excuse me. Now they are called the PO-2's. It was a sad day when Polikarpov crashed his plane. But they have honored him by calling the Biplanes that he designed after him."

"Yes, I know," she said respectfully. "I was in training when word came of his death. It is a great loss to the Motherland of such a gifted man."

"Comrade, the PO-2's can maneuver in a split second and can land and take off on almost any kind of terrain," he said studying her face. "That gives the Biplanes a slight advantage. The YAK-2's are quite different."

"I am well aware of the advantages and disadvantages of piloting a PO-2 and a YAK-1," she said almost indignantly. Elena gave a lengthy, detailed description of what the PO-2 could do and ended by saying, "Add the fact that the German's radar cannot detect the canvas sur faces of the PO-2, and it can also fly very low to the ground." She stopped, cocked her head, and looked at him.

Nikolai sat back in his chair and studied Elena for a moment before he spoke, "Yes, you know all about the PO-2, but a YAK-1 is very different..."

Elena cut off his sentence. "I did go through training Commander Sr. Major Belko," she said indignantly. "A Yakovlev or YAK-1 fighter is a low-wing aircraft with an enclosed single seat cockpit. It has two small-caliber machine guns, with a cannon attached to the fuselage. The maximum speed is 700 kilometers, which is almost twice the speed of the PO-2." She crossed her arms and pushed back on her chair and smiled confidently. "Did I forget anything?"

"You forgot about the water-cooled 1,100 HP engine in the YAK-1," he said with a twinkle in his eyes.

Elena laughed and relaxed in his presence. They stayed talking and laughing for a couple more hours until he said they had an early flight in the morning, and she needed to acclimate herself to the facility. He walked with her to her quarters, gave a courtesy nod, and walked away. Elena stood for a while watching him and then entered her new quarters.

There had been so many men who had displayed their affection and attention toward her, and none of them had piqued her interest. But there was something different, something special about Commander Sr. Major Belko.

* * *

Morning came too quickly for Elena. She felt like she could have slept for days instead of hours. Elena and Oxana quickly readied for their scheduled flights and hurried to the field toward their planes.

"About time you got here," Commander Belko said smiling down at Elena. "So are you ready?"

"Yes, Comrade Commander Sr. Major Belko," she straightened her shoulders and came to attention.

"That is good, because being my wingman means you had better be ready. And, there has been a change in our flight," he said to Elena as he showed her the map and destination. "It is reported that a large number of German planes have been attacking villages along this route. Their fighters are shooting at the people on the road who are fleeing the village. They are killing women and children. It makes no sense to me. We will be free hunting them this morning."

"Free hunting is a good thing." Elena saluted her Commander and walked toward her plane. She was startled to see men working on planes and men pilots climbing into their fighter planes. She was used to seeing only women flying and working on their planes. I hope these men are as dedicated and as good as the women, she thought climbing onto the wing.

"I checked everything out with Comrade Private Fedar." Aleksandra rolled her eyes toward Fedar, the male ground crewman, who was also assigned to Elena's plane. "I found out this morning I have been assigned as your lead mechanic."

"I can relax now knowing that my plane is in good hands," Elena smiled as she climbed into the cockpit.

Elena took nothing for granted as she checked out the working functions of her plane. After she secured her safety harnesses, and adjusted the parachute for her to sit on, Elena began her routine check of her plane. The elevator that raised and lowered her plane in flight, the rudder pedals, and the ailerons that controlled the rolling motion of her plane were all working. Comfortable that everything had checked out she gave the signal to her ground crew that she was ready for takeoff and pulled the cockpit hood tightly closed.

Aleksandra and Fedar pulled the ropes of the wooden chocks from under the plane's wheels and hurried a safe distance away from the whirling propellers.

The commander and Elena flew together for a couple of hours but found no trace of any enemy planes. Sr. Major Belko gave the signal to return to base.

Elena and Nikolai flew a couple of more times before it started to get dark. All of their flights turned out to be uneventful.

"It will not always be this easy," he said.

"I hope not," she replied.

Chapter 7

A couple of months later, Elena and Oxana strolled toward their planes to begin their day by free hunting for German bombers.

"I find this runway very bumpy," Oxana complained.

"Bumpy? You think this is bumpy?" Elena laughed. "We had nothing like this to land on."

She peered down at the landing strip they were walking on. The runway area was leveled and covered with octagonal concrete, paving slabs that interlocked giving it a honeycomb-looking effect. "It has to be a pain to keep picking up these concrete slabs and moving them from base to base. But it is better than landing on a grassy, muddy field."

"Absolutely, especially when we are taking off and landing in the rain. I wish the whole field was paved. I guess it will suffice as a runway. But we have to park our planes off to the side of it and sometimes in the deep mud." Oxana complained as she approached her plane.

"Like last week," Elena shook her head. "It took six of us to try to push one plane onto the runway."

"It is a good thing you thought of having the trucks pull the planes out of the mud. What a mess that day was," Oxana reached her plane and waved at Elena as she climbed in. "On the bright side, we now have two-way radios."

"See you up there," Elena waved back and smiled.

The sky was clear with just a smattering of clouds drifting lazily above them as they flew their fighters into the crisp, cold air. Elena adjusted the oxygen mask over her nose and mouth. The smell of rubber and leather filled her nostrils along with the cool stream of oxygen. "Climbing to 6000 feet." Elena spoke into her new two-way radio.

"Copy that," Oxana responded.

Both women flew at the high altitude for a while when Elena broke their solitude. "Enemy bombers 5000 feet. Nine O'clock."

"Lots of them," Oxana replied. "They seem to be heading toward Moscow."

"Base control." Elena called on her radio. "We are engaging numerous enemy Heinkel III bombers." She quickly gave their location to base headquarters.

Elena and Oxana knew that there was a weak spot on the Heinkel bomber. It was in a specific area to the rear of the plane where the bomber's machine guns were useless in a fight. "Time to do some real damage," said Elena sizing up the enemy planes.

Directly below them the enemy bombers flew in a V formation and seemed unaware of the two YAKs flying above them.

"Let's get the lead bombers," Oxana heard Elena say into her headphone.

"Let's go," said Oxana.

Instantly, they dropped down and flew over the entire bomber squadron and struck the lead bomber. Elena and Oxana split; one went right and the other left. They took out another two bombers amid the fiery blaze of bullets the German gunners were now throwing at them.

Elena and Oxana were circling around for another strike when two Messerschmitts flipped out from under the bombers and flew straight toward them. Both women were firing their front machine guns at the oncoming Messerschmitt fighters, and they were returning fire.

Elena and Oxana swerved and swayed in the air to keep their planes from being hit. The four planes were flying at each other in a head-on collision course. The German fighter planes kept coming toward them, as the women held their course. At the last second the two Messerschmitts broke off. One veered to the right and one to the left: It was a fatal move on their part. Elena veered to the right coming in directly behind one Messerschmitt, and Oxana did the same with the other one that veered to the left.

It was over in seconds. Elena and Oxana strafed and destroyed the enemy planes they were chasing. They quickly swung their planes around just in time to see reinforcements from their base camp heading toward them.

The German bombers saw the support planes flying in and turned their planes to head back toward German occupied territories.

"Moscow thanks you," Elena laughed over her headphone as the bombers headed away from Moscow.

"And we thank you," Oxana chimed in.

"Nice work, Comrades," a Soviet pilot spoke over his radio.

"Excellent is more like it," Nikolai said. "Keep alert for other enemy fighters or bombers."

Several weeks went by as Elena and Oxana fought alone and alongside of the male pilots and soon had the respect of everyone. The base commander was so impressed with their bravery and flying abilities that he put in orders for the two women Ace pilots to be named Heroes of the Soviet Union.

Their air base had been moved a couple of times during the last couple of weeks, and the living arrangements changed as much as their location.

Elena walked into her new underground, make-shift quarters, and found Oxana doing needle point. She walked over and looked down at the blue pattern of flowers that Oxana was making. "Oh, that is very pretty," Elena said admiring her work.

"Thank you," Oxana said pulling a blue thread through the top of the cloth.

"Aren't you tired? I am so tired I can barely keep my eyes open." She took the two steps to her cot and flopped down on it.

"No, I was just relaxing before I go out and do some free hunting. The Germans have been sending a lot of bombers toward Moscow lately. Maybe I can catch them off guard." Oxana carefully pushed the needle up through the material.

"Talk about being caught off guard. I noticed you were having a very, very good time last night." She looked over at Oxana, who had a silly smirk inching across her face.

"Umm, well, yes I had a very good time," Oxana giggled.

"In the months I have known you I have never, and I repeat, never heard you giggle. It did not have anything to do with Senior Lieutenant Rolan Durisovka, did it?" Elena shot a sly look at Oxana and smiled.

"Could be," she said.

Her tone to Elena was of someone trying to sound nonchalant. "He is very tall, and very smart."

"Yes. Yes, he is," Oxana jabbed her needle into the material, and then stopped and looked at Elena. "He was in the University studying to be a physicist, before he became a pilot. We have been seeing each other for a month now."

"Dear Oxana, the man is very smitten with you," Elena threw her head back and laughed. "He showed no interest in anyone but you at the party."

Oxana put down her needle point and pulled the blanket from her lap. "I have a real interest in him as well," she smiled broadly. "Can you imagine someone as big as me having a beau?"

"Of course," Elena looked over at her best friend and smiled. "Once they get to know you they can see the beauty that you really are."

"You are just saying that because you are my friend. But do not stop, I like hearing that and maybe someday I will believe it." She laughed and stood up. "Sr. Lt. Rolan Durisovka and I are doing some free hunting together today." Oxana arched her back and softly moaned. "You rest, because you have been flying all morning. I will fill you in on Sr. Lt. Rolan when I get back."

* * *

Elena was awakened by someone calling her name through the canvas door of her dugout quarters. Groggily, she pulled the blanket off and stumbled toward the door. She pulled back the canvas and was startled to see Nikolai standing there. "You cannot come in here," she exclaimed in shock.

"Elena," his voice was as serious as his face.

"What? What is it?" Elena was still trying to wake up.

"Oxana and Rolan were shot down earlier today."

The blood drained from her face, "Are ... are they alive somewhere?"

"No," he lowered his head. "They found their bodies near their planes."

"But how? This cannot be. She is an excellent pilot," Elena gasped. She still could not believe that her friend was gone.

"From what they could tell, at least three Messerschmitts were shot down along with them. It looks like they put up a fierce fight. They must have been greatly outnumbered."

"Where ... are they now?" She couldn't bring herself to ask where her body was taken, because there was such finality to it; no hope.

"They recovered them and took them to the nearest base," he said gently.

Elena threw back her head and screamed, "No! No!" She began to sob uncontrollably. Nikolai swiftly took her into his arms. After a while, she pulled away from him and looked up into his face. Her eyes were reddened and swollen from crying. "I want to fly now!"

"Elena you have been on duty for eight hours and have only had a couple of hours of sleep." He held her gently by her shoulders.

"I am awake now," she spat out. "I want to kill those fascist animals now."

"Gear up," he said. "We will fly as soon as you are ready." He turned and walked up out of the shelter.

She grabbed her gear and hurried toward the flapping tarp that covered her doorway. She stopped and looked down at the almost finished needle point that Oxana had been working on and grabbed it.

Nikolai was waiting by his plane and nodded to her as they climbed into their planes and headed down the make-shift airstrip.

Elena's face was streaked from the tears that had poured down her face. She placed the needle point Oxana had been working on near the dashboard. Her tears had dried up, and her body was filled with fierce determination. She was ready to exact her revenge.

They flew for a while when Nikolai's voice broke the silence, "Squadron of German bombers six o'clock at 5000 feet. They have protection. Four Messers."

"Only four?" Elena's voice filled with hatred. "Stupid fascists. They should have sent a hundred to protect them."

"Time for fun." He dove down and took out one of the unsuspecting Messerschmitts. He quickly called in his location to base headquarters asking for reinforcements.

Elena dove straight down for the lead bomber and destroyed it. She swung up and banked a hard-right shooting down one of the second enemy Messers that was trying to circle around and attack her.

She was unaware of the third plane coming in from behind her when Nikolai yelled into his radio transmitter, "Behind you!" His attention was diverted back to his own battle with the fourth enemy pilot.

Elena looked behind her and saw the fiery flash of the fighter guns. She pulled a hard left. The bullets hit her wing but did not stop her flying power. She climbed into the sky and circled around with the enemy following her every step. Elena swayed back and forth making it harder for the pilot to achieve a direct hit. She could hear the bullets as they pierced the wings of her plane. Some of the bullets came very close to her in the cabin, striking the edge of her seat. Then she did something that the German pilot was not expecting.

She cut her engines, pulled back on the throttle and let her plane drop like a rock. The Messerschmitt flew over her, and immediately she kicked her engines on, and now she was behind it. Elena aimed her machine guns at the enemy fighter in front of her. Instantly it caught fire and exploded. The concussion from the blast caused her plane to shudder and shake, but Elena held the controls tightly, as she steered her plane out of the way of any shrapnel from the exploding plane.

She looked over and saw that Nikolai had defeated the Messerschmitt he was fighting, and now they both concentrated on taking out the enemy bombers whose trajectory seemed to be headed straight for Moscow again.

Minutes later, the sky was filled with Soviet fighters. The German squadron of bombers veered off and headed away from the pursuing Soviet fighters.

They chased the retreating bombers, destroying many of them, until they had to stop, because they knew that the German bombers would have called for their fighter planes to come and protect them. The Soviet planes would have stayed to fight them, but they were running out of gas and ammunition.

Elena landed her plane and taxied off the landing strip. Aleksandra was there waiting for her; her eyes red from crying. Both women hugged each other for a moment.

"Did you get them?" Aleksandra's voice was filled with grief for their lost friend Oxana.

"Not enough of them," she said pulling away. "They should fear, because I will be back up there searching for them."

Chapter 8

The German General was seated at his desk when the colonel knocked on his open door.

"Come, come," the general said impatiently.

"Here are the dispatches, Herr General." The young officer handed the file folder to him.

The general pushed his glasses back to the bridge of his long nose. He opened the folder and read each sheet carefully placing those he read face down on the desk. One sheet caused him to grimace. As he continued to read the report, his blue eyes narrowed, and his heavy jaw tightened. "Women bombers? Women bomber pilots? These are the pilots who are creating hell for our men on the ground. That cannot be. Women bomber pilots?"

"Yes, Herr General." The colonel stood with his back straight. His pale, blue eyes avoided direct contact with the general's angry eyes.

"Are they sure these Biplanes are being flown by women? Maybe it is their men dressed as women to make us think their women are these resilient bombers." The general's eyes moved back and forth as he tried to think of a reason these Biplanes were being so effectively flown by mere women. "Of course, that is it. They are men dressed as women."

"Herr General, our ground troops have gathered this information from capturing some of the women pilots and from the Russian towns-people in cities near Moscow. Our troops say when they fly, they make a sound like a witch's broom. They call them Night Witches."

"This report says they are flying old World War I Biplanes. We have top notch pilots, and they cannot shoot down these women?" He looked up in disgust, "Women flying antiquated, and I repeat, antiquated Biplanes and our finest pilots cannot shoot these women out of the sky. Tell me why?" His voice changed to a warning, more than a question.

"Our fighters are too fast and cannot fly low enough to engage them. The Biplanes fly very low and slow and have great maneuverability. When our..."

The general cut him off, "I know what a Biplane is and what it can do," he snapped. "I want to know why our pilots are not shooting them out of the sky."

"I do not know, General." The colonel said meekly.

The general's face lit up. "Ah, it says here that recently one of our fighter planes downed four of these night creatures. I want that pilot given the Iron Cross medal. In fact, any of our pilots who destroy one of these ... these night witches will receive our highest honor."

"Yes, Herr General." The colonel remained at attention looking straight ahead.

The general sat there thinking and drumming his fingers on the desktop. Finally, he looked up into the colonel's face. "I do not understand why they have sent women to fight in those death traps." He paused for a moment in thought. "Of course," he said nodding his head. "They must be criminals who have done a hideous crime, and this is their punishment."

The colonel's face remained stoic as the general sat back in his chair. He waited patiently until the general returned to the rest of the dispatches he had brought.

After each paper the general flipped over, he nodded and grunted. Until he got to the last dispatch sent. "A woman?" He said incredulously. "This says there is a fierce woman pilot who has been shooting down our Ace pilots." He took off his glasses and threw them on top of his desk. "There are women fighter pilots, too?" He asked incredulously. "Did we kill off all their men, and do not know it?"

"General," he replied. "It has been reported that the morale of the men is becoming very low."

"Find her and eliminate her," the general snarled. "Flowers painted on the side of her plane," he huffed in disgust and threw the sheet of paper onto his desk.

"Yes, General," he nodded. "She has blue flowers painted on her plane for every one of our pilots she shoots down."

"Yes, I have read that. I want her found and killed. That is a priority. I will issue that order immediately," he shouted. He picked up the piece of paper off his desk, shook his head, crumpled up the paper, and threw it in the wastebasket by the side of his desk. "I want all efforts to find that bitch and kill her." He looked up at the soldier and glared. "Wait outside my office until I have the orders prepared. You are excused."

"Yes, Herr General," he saluted, clicked his heels and hurried from the room.

The general sat in thought for a moment. "Women bombers and pilots. What good do they think they can do? They are just weak woman playing at war. They do not have the instinct and stamina of a man. So far, they have escaped by sheer luck. That ends now. I will increase anti-aircraft cannons, search lights and have them post several lookouts at all bases. Their elimination will be an easy one. The Furher will be inspired by my solution and actions to rid our country of these pesky, ridiculous women."

Chapter 9

Elena and Nikolai fought together in battle after battle, each protecting one another, and their fellow pilots. The few times that Nikolai was away at a field meeting, Elena would free hunt alone for any fascist activity in the sky. She had become known as the Lone Wolf and would patrol the skies by herself.

One afternoon after scouting for enemy planes, Elena got into a fierce fight with two Messerschmitts. She outwitted them at every turn and downed them, but not before they damaged her plane. She headed back to base with a black trail of smoke coming from the rear of her plane.

Elena struggled to get control of the throttle. But her biggest problem was the rudder pedals. Because she was so short, a box had been fitted so that she could reach the pedals with her foot. A bullet had smashed into the little box and grazed her leg. She had to unbuckle her safety lines and stand to maneuver the plane, so she could land it.

She did not notice that the landing field was littered with people standing around. Elena was oblivious to the wound on her leg; she was too preoccupied with landing safely. Her plane hit the ground hard. It swerved and jerked, as she desperately pulled back on the throttle to keep the plane's nose up.

Elena managed to guide her plane away from the other planes. She did not want her plane exploding around anyone or any parked planes on the airfield.

A team of soldiers were already en route to her. A couple of soldiers pulled her out, while others checked to see if the plane could be saved. It was unanimous; it could not be saved. They put her in their truck and sped away from the smoking aircraft.

Elena was headed for the medic's quarters when a mob of people charged the truck.

"Stop! Stop!" A woman screamed at the driver of the truck. "We need to talk with her."

The driver came to a stop, and everyone rushed to the back of the truck where Elena was sitting. Not knowing what was going on Elena got out of the truck and faced the group of people in front of her.

"What is all of this?"

"Ah, are you the female Ace pilot we have heard so much about?" A man with a long, bearded face said, more than asked.

"You are much prettier in person," said a female with too much make-up and wearing a tight dress.

"Who are you people?" Elena snapped. "What do you want?"

"We are the people of the Soviet press, and we were told of your exploits and want to know all about you." The bearded-faced man bristled for a moment and with disappointment asked Elena. "Why did you land that plane? You should have crashed landed. My camera was ready for an explosion, and you spoiled the whole thing. It would have made for a much better story."

"Get away from me," Elena was so shocked and sickened by what he said she had the urge to punch him.

"We are going to make you the heroine of the Soviet Union." The woman with too much make-up said.

"I said get away from me," Elena growled. "Every pilot in the Red Army is a hero. And, the ground crews are the unsung heroes."

"Comrade, they do not look like you," the female reporter almost purred to Elena.

"Please just leave me alone." Elena tried looking for a way to get past them.

The woman leaned in close to Elena and spoke quickly. "Well, comrade, you have caught the eye of General Hrtova. He said a beauty like you would be a beacon to all young men and women to come forth and serve our Motherland. And, he wants you to go on tour with him throughout our great country and lift up the spirits of our people." She grabbed Elena's arm and whispered in her ear, "He said to tell you that you would be treated well if you play along, if you know what I mean." She pulled back and winked at Elena.

"I have never met this General Hrtova," Elena snapped.

"He was at your base briefly and caught sight of you. He began asking questions about you and concluded that you would be a very good propaganda source for our Motherland."

"I am not interested," Elena said coldly.

"Enough," Nikolai's strong, male voice boomed out as he pushed his way next to Elena. He looked down and saw the blood spattered on Elena's pant leg. "Are you all so stupid you cannot see she has been wounded?" He gently took Elena's arm and led her away from startled press directly to the medical compound.

After her wound was cleaned and dressed, they walked out of the dugout to be surrounded by the Soviet press again. Cameras were flashing, and the reporters kept throwing questions at her.

Suddenly, the presses' attention was diverted by a plane catching fire as it landed on the airfield.

Elena grabbed Nikolai's hand, "I know a place. It is my own private place. Come on."

Elena and Nikolai raced into the woods behind their quarters; disappearing. They ran until they came to a fallen tree nestled deep in the forest and sat down on it.

A safe distance away from the gawking reporters, Elena began telling Nikolai what the Soviet press had said.

Panic gripped Elena, "Nikolai. I do not want to be sent away to be paraded around like a pet monkey."

"I agree, but," he stopped.

"But, what?" she asked.

"But I would know you would be safe," he looked away.

"I do not want to be safe. I want to fight to free our Motherland and to always be with you," she added and then gasped. She had never spoken her feelings for him out loud.

Nikolai turned to her slowly. "Did you say what I thought you said?"

"Which part?" Elena asked, trying to avoid the slip of her tongue. She was afraid that he did not return the feelings she had for him.

"The part where you said, 'to always be with you' comes to mind," he said.

"Are you angry that I said that?" Her voice filled with worry.

"Angry? My dear, dear Elena, when I saw the press surrounding you, I was very upset. But when I saw that you were wounded, and they were blocking your way to the medical center I was outraged." Gently, he took one of her hands in his. "I wanted to grab you in my arms and kiss you and never stop. And, I would have if the idiot Soviet press was not around."

"You would have?" She asked incredulously.

"Of course, I would," he put his hand over his heart. "I think I would know something like that. Too bad the press was there, or you would have found out for yourself."

Nikolai moved his hand and placed it over hers. "I must ask you something."

"What?" She asked.

"Why have you no man in your life?"

"Because I have never met one that I felt I could look up to and trust with my heart," Elena said seriously. "Until," she said playfully, knowing he would want to hear what 'until' meant. She didn't have to wait long.

"Until? You did not finish that sentence, until what?"

Elena laughed with all the joy her heart could hold, "Until I met you, my love."

Nikolai closed his eyes and threw back his head with a deep sigh. He lowered his head and looked into her eyes. "I love you Elena. I love you with a depth that knows no end."

* * *

A couple of months passed by and Elena and Nikolai were almost inseparable in battle and on the ground. Elena knew this was the man she would love for as long as she lived.

On a cool April evening, Nikolai led Elena to their favorite spot in the forest. They stood before the fallen tree trunk and kissed one another with a passion that seemed to consume them. Nikolai finally broke the kiss and stared into her beautiful face. He ran his thumb over her jaw line and leaned down to kiss her forehead. He pulled her to him and held her tightly in his arms. "This morning we had a very difficult fight. I am worried about you. Those German fighters seemed to zero in on you."

"Nikolai, they were trying to get at you, and I was just in the way," she snuggled deeper into his arms.

"No, I sensed something else. One of them had a clear shot at me and dove down to fire at you." He shook his head and rubbed his chin on top of her head.

"Well, I bet he was surprised when I shot him down," she laughed and pulled away. "You know I am a fighter pilot, and that is what I do."

"My love, look at your plane. It has more bullet holes than the rest of our planes. It just does not make any sense." Nikolai reached down, gently putting his hands on her waist, picked her up, and placed her on the fallen tree trunk.

"I just stick my nose into everyone else's business," she wrinkled her nose at him.

He moved to sit next to her. "You are an excellent pilot, my love, one of the best. I think you are my good-luck charm."

"We must always be together," she said looking over at him.

"We will always be together. I promise, even if I was to die, I would wait for you. Would you not wait for me?" he smiled and put his arm around her shoulders.

"Do not talk of dying," Elena turned her head so that he could not see the tears forming in her eyes. "We must not talk of dying."

"My love," he said gently. "We fly toward death every day. It is always a possibility."

"No, not for us," she turned looking into his face. "Not for us. We are real and full of life. Breathe the air in. Do you not feel it in your lungs? Do you feel alive? I do. We have so much to live for."

Gently, he pulled her closer to him. His arms tightened around her. "Yes. Yes, we have much to live for," he said softly.

She pulled away from him and looked into his face, "I would give my life for you and the Motherland."

"And I for you and the Motherland." He stared hard at her for a moment and then said, "Enough of this morbid talking. I have a thought. Would you like to hear it?"

"Of course," she said smiling at him.

"I have been thinking that we should marry."

"I think that is wonderful thinking," Elena jumped off the log. "Today."

"I already have the paperwork and everything else prepared. The base commander has agreed to marry us. I think today would be a good day," he said kissing her again.

"I love you Nikolai. I love you with every breath my body takes," Elena looked up into his face and began to chuckle. "I want to have six children and cook you wonderful meals. And I want to build our house right here in the forest. Right here on this very spot, where I have been the happiest I have ever been in my life. We will be here forever, together."

"Wait?" He feigned shock. "You can cook?" Nikolai asked in a surprised voice.

"No," she laughed. "But, for you I will learn."

"It is done," he said sounding serious. "We will have six children, build our home here, and you will learn to cook so that I may have wonderful meals when I come home from work. And, we will live here forever, together." He paused for a moment, "But I want you to do something for me."

"Anything, just ask," she pulled back from his strong and comforting embrace.

"Practice on someone else until you have learned to cook," he said teasingly.

"Oh, you," she said playful punching his arm.

He took her back in his embrace, and his voice became serious. "I love you Elena. My darling, brave, little Elena. I, too, have never known such happiness until I met you."

"You did not think so when we first met," she snuggled deeper into his arms.

"No, no. I was just shocked to see such a beautiful woman walk into my command center." He pulled her back and looked at her, "The moment I saw you; I fell in love. And the more I got to know you the larger my love grew for you – if that is even possible."

* * *

They were married that evening, and the entire regiment helped to celebrate their union by throwing a party. It was not a fancy party, but someone managed to find some Vodka and a record player. Then, the base commander said as a gift to them on their wedding day they could both take the day off tomorrow, and he was lending them his private quarters for the night. He told them he was being flown to a meeting that night and would not be back until the day-after tomorrow, which would give them the whole day by themselves in his quarters.

Nikolai and Elena laughed and danced with everyone until it was suggested that it was time for the two of them to leave. The couple said their good-byes to everyone and thanked them for the spontaneous and wonderful wedding party.

The next-day Elena found a basket filled with food and drinks for them at the front door of the base commander's quarters No one saw them for the remainder of the day.

Early the next morning they were awakened to fly their surveillance over the countryside. They dressed, gave each other one last kiss, and headed toward their planes.

Aleksandra and the other mechanic were shaking their heads as they stood by Elena's plane.

Nikolai and Elena walked over to them.

"I am sorry, Comrade Sr. Lieutenant, your plane, that is only a couple of months old, has been too badly damaged to fly today. How you managed to fly it back to the airfield I have no idea. We have been working on it for a couple of days. I will be lucky to get it ready for you by tomorrow. Comrade Private Fedar made you another pedal box, but the fuselage has been hit, and the engine is a mess."

"Then find me another plane," Elena ordered.

"Comrade Sr. Lt., these are the only planes we have," Fedar said. "We cannot just snap our fingers and one will appear."

"Do not speak to my Senior Lieutenant like that or I will box your ears," Aleksandra huffed. "Now get that engine out so we can repair it, Comrade Private Fedar."

"Yes, Comrade Corporal," he said with defeat registering in his voice.

"There are a couple of fighter planes coming in today. If he cannot get your plane fixed by tomorrow, I will make sure you have a new one when I get back." Nikolai winked and walked away from her toward his plane. He climbed into his plane, smiled and waved at her. "I will be lost without my wingman."

He flew his plane into the sky and circled back around the landing field, waggled his wings, and flew off into the grey clouds looming overhead.

Elena threw him a kiss and waved frantically until he disappeared into the dense clouds above. Suddenly, Elena grabbed her throat. She felt something bad was going to happen. She wanted to fly after him and bring him back, but all she could do was stand there staring helplessly into the gray, cloudy sky until he disappeared from her view.

A few more fighter planes took off following Nikolai's plane. Elena sighed. Knowing that he wouldn't be up there alone made her feel a little less anxious.

Elena waited anxiously on the airfield checking out her plane's dashboard, fuel lines, anything that would take her mind off Nikolai.

Aleksandra, still working on Elena's plane, called out to her, "Comrade Senior Lieutenant, I have to be out here in this cold; you do not. Warm yourself in your quarters. I will have someone come and get you when his plane returns."

The warmth from the kerosene heater could not penetrate the cold fear she felt for Nikolai. She had paced back and forth in their quarters until she could bear it no longer and hurried to the airfield to wait for his return.

Soon, the droning sound of airplane engines could be heard heading toward their base. Elena's heart was beating wildly as she waited until the planes cleared the tree line, and she could count them. She gasped. One plane was missing. One plane. She watched solemnly as each plane landed. Some planes were so crippled they could barely reach the landing. Smoke poured out of a couple of the planes, as it hit the ground with no landing gear down.

Elena looked for Nikolai's plane, and fear gripped her heart. His plane was missing. She ran to the first plane that had landed and waited until he descended. "Comrade Commander Nikolai's plane. Where is it?" She commanded.

"His plane was shot down by the river. But I saw him parachute out," the pilot shook his head. "Commander Nikolai saved us by maneuvering behind the German planes and taking out a couple of them. Then a ME came in from behind him and shot his plane down. We fought a long time before they managed to get away."

"Why didn't you go after him? Where is Nikolai?" She screamed at the other pilots.

"We didn't go after him because we were out of gas and ammo." His voice filled with anger. "Do you not think we would have brought him back if we could have?"

Elena turned and ordered one of the mechanics. "Fuel me a plane that can fly, now!"

"They have all been shot up," the mechanic said.

"Can that plane fly?" She yelled pointing to the last plane that had just landed.

"Yes, but it may not be safe," he replied.

"I do not care. Get it fueled now! Get the ammo loaded! Aleksandra get my pillows and pedal box from my plane, quickly."

A couple of the other pilots whose planes could fly had theirs refueled and their ammunition refilled, too.

After Elena's pedal box was attached, she jumped into the pilot seat and roared down the runway with two other pilots right behind her. One of the pilots took the lead and headed for the area they had last seen their commander.

The lead pilot waggled his wings and turned his plane toward an open grassy field below. The bright white of a parachute hung eerily among the dark, barren branches of a tree.

Elena landed her plane and jumped out running and yelling Nikolai's name. She got to the tree and stopped at the sight before her. Nikolai's body was riddled with bullets and hung suspended in the tree like a grotesque Christmas ornament. Elena stood there for a moment in shock. Nikolai was dead. Her love was dead. This could not be real.

Finally, the shock wore off and the pain took over in an intensity she had never felt before. Her body shook as the anguish overtook her. She fell to her knees looking up at Nikolai's lifeless body. She began screaming and wailing as her body weaved back and forth.

One of the pilots climbed the tree and released Nikolai' body from the parachute entangled in the tree branches. When his body slumped to the ground Elena grabbed him up in her arms rocking him, sobbing and kissing his face. She raised her head and screamed in uncontrollable agony.

Gently, one of the pilots pried her arms from around the dead commander's body. "We must go. The Germans are near this area."

"I do not care," she sobbed. "I want to die here with him."

"You must live to fight the Germans who did this to him," the pilot's voice was soft but firm. "He would want you to do that for him and the Motherland."

Elena did not remember getting into her plane. She did not remember the trip back to base or even landing her plane.

She had Nikolai buried by their favorite spot in the forest. After everyone had left she sat a long time staring at the mound of dirt that covered her love. She walked over to the mound and threw herself on top of it and cried until darkness began to creep across the land.

Elena got up from the dirt that covered her Nikolai. She didn't bother to brush herself off. She walked to the field where her plane was sitting. Aleksandra was still there working on her plane. She looked up and saw Elena, "I am sorry…"

Elena waved her hand to silence her. Elena did not want anyone mentioning his name or giving their condolences. She did not want to think about his death. Right now, all she wanted to do was to kill the Hitlerites who did this to him. "Will my plane be ready by tomorrow?"

"Yes," was the weak reply from Aleksandra.

For the next week, Elena attacked and destroyed with a vengeance, every German plane that came within her sight. She outmaneuvered and outflew any plane they threw at her. They were almost running out of space to paint the flowers on her plane.

Elena and the other pilots were told of a new patrol of German planes that was bombing and strafing a village about twenty kilometers away. The Germans were getting to close to their landing field, and they had to stop them from advancing any further, and to try to protect the village.

It was a gray day, and the morning mist hung like a shroud over the airfield as they climbed into their planes. Elena and four other pilots headed into the cloudy, dismal sky. They flew in the direction where the enemy planes were last sighted. The clouds were dense and low to the ground as they flew into them.

Elena thought she saw movement in the clouds to her right. She radioed the other pilots and advised she was going to check out possible enemy bombers. She veered off alone and headed straight into the clouds. Unable to find anything she pushed down and surfaced just below the clouds. "Seems all clear," she radioed.

Suddenly, out of nowhere several German fighter planes broke through the clouds. Elena was outnumbered six to one and the three

Russian pilots who had accompanied her were nowhere to be seen. "I am under attack," she radioed. Six Messers."

Elena climbed back up through the clouds and then dove down, but to no avail as they chased after her. She out maneuvered one of the enemy fighters and shot him down. And, then, off in a distance she saw her comrades racing toward the fight.

Suddenly, bullets ripped through Elena's plane striking her in the stomach and shoulder. The pain was intense, but she didn't scream. Her thoughts were on taking out her enemy. She turned and flipped her plane sideways. Bloodied and in pain, she shot down another attacker, when several rounds of bullets swept through her plane. Her plane erupted into flames. The flames greedily consumed the needlepoint that Oxana had been working on that hung on a bolt in Elena's cockpit.

Elena no longer felt any pain. A white light began growing around her, and then Nikolai was there with his hand outstretched to her. "I waited for you like I promised. Come, my love," he said. Elena heaved one last breath as her plane twisted and turned until it smashed into the ground below.

Chapter 10

When Vera heard about the tragic news of the deaths of Elena and Nikolai, she was deeply distraught. She sat on her cot and wept for both. They were like a beautiful candle of hope against all the ugliness war had brought with it. Villagers found Elena's body and had her brought to the airfield. Elena was buried next to Nikolai in the forest where they first told each other of their love.

* * *

A couple of weeks later, after a long night of bombings, Vera climbed out of her shot up plane. Larissa and Rimma shook their heads at the bullet ridden condition of her plane.

"This is some welcome back, Comrade Ksenia," Rimma shook her head. "I think this is a record for holes in your plane."

"We will be up all-night making repairs on this," Larissa said. "But you two will not be flying again tonight. Look at that fog."

"I have no idea how you made it back here. There is absolutely no visibility for anyone to fly." Rimma raised her hand and patted the side of the plane.

"It was all Comrade Vera this time. I fell asleep," Ksenia smiled sleepily.

Vera patted Ksenia's arm. "I am very glad to have you back."

"We are, too," Rimma said and yawned.

"You two get some rest," Larissa moved under the plane and began inspecting for more damage. "You made ten trips and that is enough I would think."

"You two could use some rest as well," Vera said.

"You cannot see to fly, but unfortunately, we can see very well up close, so we have to keep working," Rimma said climbing onto the wing. "Go."

Vera gave a slight smile, waved good-bye, and headed for her new quarters that were now dugouts in the ground. She was startled to see four new faces as she entered through the canvas door.

A tall, buxom, very pretty, blond strode toward her and nodded. "I am Corporal Katrina Navokovich. One of your new navigators."

"Yes, she is," sighed a pugged nose woman sitting on a cot. Her brown eyes narrowed slightly. "She has more energy than a bee in a flower patch." She gestured with her head at the two other women in the shelter and introduced them and then herself, "Senior Lieutenant Polina Grovlonova."

"Senior Captain Vera Zhkov. Welcome to our fancy abode."

"I have heard of your recent promotion. Congratulations." She nodded to Vera.

"Thank you," said Vera. "Our Commander Voskolov has also been promoted. She now is a Major." Vera stopped and looked at Katrina. "What is she doing?" she asked watching the bubbly Katrina, who was busy boiling water on their make-shift stove.

Polina looked at Vera and shrugged, "Boiling water to wash our hair."

"I wish the pot was much larger," Vera took off her jacket and placed it on her cot. "What I would give for a bath right now." She smelled of diesel fuel; her face had grease on it, and her head itched from being dirty.

"Oh," Katrina turned toward Vera, "the water truck will be here in two days."

"Two days?" Vera asked somewhat surprised. "How do you know this?"

"She should be a spy instead of a navigator. She can find out more things than all of us put together." Polina dropped her feet onto the dirt floor. "We are just out of flight school," she said looking around at their meager dwellings. "Are these normal quarters for pilots and navigators? It is damp, smelly and very cramped. And there is only one makeshift-toilet on the entire base."

"Tell us something we do not already know. Although sometimes we are billeted in a house, but that is rare," Vera sat down on her bunk.

"But we are below ground and there is nothing to stop the rain and elements coming in through that ridiculous so-called door." Polina walked over to the large piece of canvas covering the opening and peered out.

"Does this place ever flood?" Katrina asked curiously.

"Only when it rains or the snow melts," Vera said.

"Do you get wet?" Katrina asked seriously.

Polina rolled her eyes and walked over to the kerosene stove to get warm. "Now you see what I have been putting up with for the last few weeks."

"It does flood Comrade," Vera shrugged slightly. "If we are lucky, they will send the pumps that day, or the next day, to get the water out."

"One time when the snow melted, we had so much water it reached over the top of our beds," Ksenia said flopping down on her bed.

"But what did you do?" Katrina's eyes widened.

"We were sleeping at the time and got very, very wet." Vera fell back against the dirt wall and smiled. "These dugouts are so comfortable," she said wryly.

"I do not find them comfortable. Hmm," Katrina's face lit up. "Then we must dance and have fun before we get very, very wet," She took the hot water off the stove and poured it into a large pail half full of cold water sitting next to the stove. "It is fortunate that you all have such short hair," Katrina said taking off her woolen cap letting her long hair fall down her back. "Your hair will dry faster."

"How did you get to keep your long hair?" Ksenia asked in shock.

"I remember someone in our training class putting up a fuss because they were told they had to cut their hair," Polina looked over at Katrina.

"Well, of course I made a fuss," Katrina said. "It is a beautiful color is it not."

"Yes. Yes, it is quite a beautiful color," Vera said looking at Katrina's light, golden hair.

"Our comrade Katrina here was the only one who did not cut her hair. She thought keeping that thick mass of gold under a cap would fool everyone. A general was inspecting our regiment, and he noticed the cap she was wearing and told her to take it off."

"I was very frightened that he was going to send me to Siberia, but he did not," Katrina smiled playfully.

Polina sighed deeply, "He thought it was a ridiculous order that women should cut their hair. He felt women should look like women not boys, and told Katrina she could keep her beautiful hair, but keep it up in a cap while on duty."

"Yes, that is what he said," she pulled her long hair over her shoulder and stroked it.

Vera laughed. "Good, so that will mean that we do not have to cut our hair anymore either. Mine is shoulder length, and I have been waiting for orders to get it cut. That is a relief to those of us who like our hair long."

An hour later, everyone had washed their hair and were sitting around the stove.

"So, tell me what you did before you went to military training, Comrade Katrina?" Vera asked.

"I worked with my parents and five older brothers on a collective farm. I am very strong. Look, I have got big muscles, just like my brothers," she said flexing her arms. "I like keeping strong. I lift many heavy things at the farm."

"Yes, you do have very strong-looking arms," Vera said smiling. "Why did you go to the university if you liked farming so much?"

"They sent me to study agriculture to help our farm," Katrina sighed deeply. "But I hated it there. I wanted to go back to the farm and smell the fresh-cut hay and laugh every day with my family.

"That sounds wonderful," Vera said.

"Oh, it was," Katrina said enthusiastically. "But then the war came, and my two older brothers were killed at the front. So, when there was a call for women to serve in the military. I quickly joined the army." She paused for a moment and continued, "Mama and Papa did not want me to leave the university. But we must do what we can for the Motherland."

"Yes, we must. What of you, Comrade Polina?" Vera asked.

Polina dropped the rag she was using to dry her hair on her lap. "I was in the university studying biology when the war came. I too felt the need to protect our Motherland."

Vera questioned the other two women in their unit, and soon all the women were conversing and enjoying each other's company.

Suddenly, Katrina jumped up and ran to her bed. She produced a very large box and opened it. Everyone gasped and laughed when she pulled out an old record player. "Come let us dance," Katrina said putting on a record called Hills of Manchzhuria.

"Oh, I love this song," one of the other women yelled, and jumped to her feet.

"Yes, of course," Katrina said as she whirled and twirled to the music. "And they will play this at the dance as well."

"How do you know all of this?" Vera asked.

"Because this is the band's favorite song to play," Katrina stopped twirling for a moment. "The dance is this coming Saturday, and I have already got us a truck to take us into the nearby town."

"Have you cleared this with the base commander?" Vera looked around the room at the women dancing and laughing.

"Yes. Yes, I have," Katrina laughed and began to twirl and dance to the music.

Everyone laughed, danced and talked late into the night.

During the next few nights, the women's sorties were increased even more, as they bombed the encroaching German troops. On the afternoon before they were supposed to start their sorties the pilots and navigators were called to their regiment commander for a briefing.

Major Voskolov stood around a piece of plank wood that she used as her table. "The fascists have figured out our line of attack, and we have to change it or none of you will be returning back to base camp tonight or any other night."

The kerosene heater and two small kerosene lamps were the only light in her quarters. The women crowded together trying to get a view of the map spread out on the tabletop.

"Your usual flight pattern on a sortie would be likened to a long, narrow loop. I estimated that we are attacking the Germans about every ten to fifteen minutes. That will change to about every three to five minutes."

The women waited to hear her explanation.

"Here is what is going to change," she looked from face to face at the young women standing around the table. "In a couple of days, we are going to have several more flight and ground crews and planes. You are all senior officers and will explain all of this to our new groups when they arrive. You are going to be flying three abreast. Two of the planes will draw the beam of the search lights and anti-aircraft cannons fire, while the third will sneak to the darkened side and drop their bombs. Then the first pilot who has dropped her payload will circle back and become one of the two planes that fly into the direct light of the enemy. Now, the second plane, that still has its bombs will fly into the darkened areas and drop her bombs. This will be repeated until all three planes have dropped their payloads."

There was total silence from the women as they listened to their new orders. "Comrade Major. No disrespect intended here," one of the pilots spoke up, "but it almost sounds like a suicide mission."

"I believe if you fly at a higher altitude when you have to enter the attack zone and weave in and out of the beams of the search lights you will keep the gunners confused and distracted on the ground enough for the third plane to drop their payload. Is this mission understood?"

"Yes, Comrade Major," they said in unison.

"Alright," she took a pencil and began outlining their drop zone and then assigned which teams would be flying in threes.

No one spoke as they headed out of her quarters and toward their planes.

"I hope the new arrivals are going to be late," said Ksenia.

"Months late," Vera said. "It is a good idea. I just do not like having to be a decoy an extra two times every flight."

"I know, flying over the search lights and AA guns once every trip is enough for me," Ksenia said shaking her head.

"Oh, well, it is for the Motherland," Vera said trying to sound cheerful.

"And it is orders." Ksenia climbed up on the wing of their plane.

"Yes. Yes, they are orders." Vera waited until Ksenia was in her cockpit before she climbed onto the wing. "We will see how it goes when the time comes," was all she said.

Neither Vera nor Ksenia brought up the new flight maneuvers again. One of the reasons was the dangerous plan and the fear of death it evoked, and the other reason was Vera and the others were beyond exhausted. When they weren't bombing the Germans during the night, they were being used to deliver dispatches, medicines, and other items to the frontlines during the day. All the women were beyond tired, but they didn't complain.

They found themselves fighting for any moment they could grab a little sleep. Some even found themselves sleeping while flying. Recently, a couple of their planes crashed killing the pilot and navigator. The other pilots couldn't help but think it was because they were tired and fell asleep during flight.

Finally, the weather took a break from its freezing, sleeting attacks on the women. It was still bitter cold, but the night sky was crisp and clear.

On their eleventh, and last sortie of the night, Vera saw one of their planes taking a direct hit from the anti-aircraft flak. The damaged plane managed to circle around in an attempt to head back to their base. The sun was starting to rise. Vera knew they had to get back to base as fast as they could. All their little Biplanes would be in great danger flying over enemy territory in the daylight hours.

There was a loud sputtering from the damaged plane. Vera and the other pilots knew what that meant. The plane's fuselage was struck. She watched helplessly as Polina and Katrina's plane began to drop. Vera could see flames shooting out from the plane as it headed toward the ground. She was about to turn around and go back to assist the downed plane when she spotted two Messerschmitts coming toward them.

All their planes scattered in the air as the Messerschmitts began chasing them. Suddenly, four Ilyushin II Soviet fighter planes appeared and quickly shot them down.

Once Vera saw that she was safe from the German fighters, she looked down and saw that her petrol gauge gave her enough fuel to turn her plane around, and search for her downed friends.

* * *

On the ground, Polina and Katrina climbed onto their burning plane's wing and jumped down.

"That was a great landing," Katrina said to Polina.

"Any safe landing is a great landing," Polina said laughing.

"Your hands have been burned," Katrina cried out. "Let me see how badly."

"I am fine," Polina spoke quickly as she carefully pulled her burnt gloves off.

"Your hands do not look fine to me," Katrina's forehead furrowed.

"I will be fine, seriously. In a couple of days, it will be all healed." Polina abruptly changed the subject. "This is a rocky riverbed. It is frozen over so it made for a bumpy, but safe landing. Although, I thought we would never stop skidding."

"Look at all the mud. Flying from this field would be impossible," Katrina said.

"Yes, but the riverbed will be easy for someone to come and rescue us. It will give them plenty of room to land and take off. We just skidded too far onto this muddy field."

"If they come back and look for us," Katrina emphasized the word 'if.'

"That may be problematic," Polina shook her head. "They may have run out of fuel or worse. And I saw a couple of Messers heading straight for them as we were struggled to get down."

"Did we land in friendly territory or enemy?" Katrina looked around at the sparsely tree-filled forest.

"I am not sure where we landed. Luckily, this riverbed and field opened up right in front of us. Still amazed at that." Polina smiled. She turned around scanning their surroundings. "Well, we had better try and get to one of our ground units before the Germans come looking for us. Anyone could see our plane coming down on fire for miles."

"Alright, time to get going. I think the field ahead looks like it is too muddy to walk in." Katrina headed up the small ravine into the woods.

Polina looked up at Katrina, who was dodging through the trees. "The shortest distance between two points is a straight line," she hollered up to Katrina. "I would rather walk a straight line then to zigzag through the trees."

"Yes, but..." Katrina's sentence was cut short by a loud explosion and a short scream.

"Comrade Polina!" Katrina shouted. "Comrade Polina what has happened?"

She ran through the trees to the edge of the forest and saw Polina lying on the ground covered in blood. "No!" She screamed and ran to Polina's side. "No! No!" Tears streamed down Katrina's face as she looked down at the still form of her pilot and friend. "What can I do? What can I do?"

Polina moaned, and her head flopped to one side.

Katrina looked around at the field she now knew would be sprinkled with mines. Carefully she got around Polina, reached under her arms and dragged her off the field into the woods. A trail of blood followed them as she gently placed her next to a tree.

Suddenly, something struck Katrina in the head, and she fell over sideways. When she turned over and looked up there were two enemy soldiers with rifles pointed at her and Polina.

They were speaking in German, and Katrina did not understand the words they were yelling at her except for one "Nachthexen." Night Witches.

One of the soldiers slapped her hard across the face causing her cap to fall off and her long hair fall around her.

She heard the two German soldiers groaning with pleasure as they stood over her with their guns.

Then Polina moaned." One of the soldiers kept a gun pointed at Katrina while the other one walked over to Polina. He kicked her in the side and hit her in the face with the butt of his gun, and then shot her in the head.

Katrina lowered her head. They did not hear the hatred in her voice as they put their guns down, "You just make big mistake." She growled softly.

They grabbed her by the hair and pulled her away from the tree, throwing her on to the ground. One of the soldiers got on top of her pinning both of her arms to the ground, while the other soldier was trying to get her pants off.

Katrina could see the sick excitement building in them. She stared with hatred into the enemy soldier's face and watched his face change from a nasty grin to surprise, as she slowly pulled her arms off the ground. The soldier's eyes were wide with stunned disbelief at her strength as she lifted her arms which he was desperately trying to hold down.

Before he knew what was happening, Katrina broke his hold and smashed him in the face with her fist. The soldier let out a scream, releasing his hold on her as he grabbed his injured face. It gave Katrina the second she needed.

Raging inside, Katrina doubled up her fist and struck the soldier sitting on top of her again so hard he reeled back landing on the stunned soldier who was still trying to get her pants off. They both toppled off Katrina. She jumped up and kicked one of the soldiers in the head and one in the stomach as they were scrambling to get up.

One of the soldiers lunged for his gun, but she stomped on his hand before he could grab it. Now both soldiers got up screaming as they lunged for her. She did a quick sidestep causing one of the soldiers to stumble past her.

She was grabbed from behind. The soldier wrapped his arms around her pinning her arms against her body. The other soldier gained back his equilibrium. He walked over and punched her in the face and stomach.

Katrina thrust her head back hard smacking the soldier holding her in the face, and kicked the other soldier standing in front of her in the groin.

Katrina spun around. The German soldier was holding his hands to his bloody, broken nose. He dropped his hand from his face and began screaming something as he lunged toward her. Katrina doubled her fist and punched him in the throat. He bent over gasping for air. She clasped her hands together, and quickly, with all her might, struck him in the back of his head. He fell to the ground and did not move. The other soldier began stumbling toward one of the guns on the ground. Just as he picked it up, she kicked it away, and then grabbed him and rammed him head-first into a tree.

Both soldiers were on the ground and did not move. Katrina picked up one of their guns and shot them both in the head.

"That is for Polina," her voice was filled with loathing. She walked over to her friend lying dead on the ground and sat down next to her. "They will come and kill me, too. I will not let them take me prisoner." She sat for a while looking at the pistol in her hand. Slowly, she raised the pistol to her head. "You were my best friend, comrade Polina. Now, I come and join you."

Just as she was about to pull the trigger Katrina thought she heard one of their Biplanes circling overhead. She dropped the gun to her side and listened. The sound of their engines was like that of no other, and then everything went quiet. She leaned her head back against the trunk of the tree and closed her eyes for a while. A few moments later, Katrina opened her eyes and sighed. "It was probably just my wishful thinking." She picked up the gun and placed it to the side of her head, when she heard a female voice calling out her name and Polina's.

* * *

Vera saw Polina and Katrina's plane below and circled around landing close to the downed plane. Vera landed a short distance away from the burning plane. "Stay here," she ordered Ksenia, as she climbed out of the cockpit and hurried to the downed plane. It was empty. "Listen to me," she yelled to Ksenia. "If I do not return within an hour, or if you see the Hitlerites approaching, fly out of here."

Ksenia started to protest, but Vera was her commanding officer, so instead she just nodded and sighed. "I understand."

Vera walked around the plane and started calling their names, "Polina! Katrina!" There was no answer. Vera reached behind her and unsnapped her holster. She took out her pistol and started walking into the woods constantly on alert for any German patrols.

She worked her way through the barren trees until she found footprints and a trail of blood as if someone were being dragged. Cautiously, she followed the trail of blood, constantly calling their names, until she saw Polina lying on the ground and Katrina sitting with her back against a tree and a pistol in her hand. Her knees were pulled up, and her elbows rested on her knees. Around her two German soldiers were sprawled on the ground.

"Katrina! Polina!" Vera called as she rushed toward them.

Slowly, Katrina looked up at Vera, with a bruised and dirty face. Her long, blond hair fell in total disarray around her face. She let her head fall back against the trunk of the tree. "I was not strong enough to help her. I failed her," she lamented.

"Katrina, you are safe. Well, for now," Vera said nervously looking around. "What has happened?"

Katrina began speaking, but almost as if Vera wasn't there. "I was ahead of her walking among the trees. I had just stepped behind a tree when I heard an explosion. Polina stepped on a land mine. I hurried back to her. She was so bloody. I dragged her away from the open field and into the trees. Polina was still alive. Her eyes were closed, but she was moaning." Finally, it seemed as if Katrina recognized Vera for the first time.

Vera looked over at the still body of Polina and at the two dead German soldiers. "We must get you out of here," she asked softly.

"I will not leave my friend, Polina," Katrina said vehemently.

"Hello! I am here!" It was Galina, a pilot from another division, that Vera knew well.

"Comrade Galina," Vera sighed audibly. "I am so glad to see you. How did you find us?"

"I was delivery papers to a general at the front and on my way back I saw a burning plane on the ground and another plane sitting nearby it. I knew it was one of ours, so I landed to see if I could help. Your navigator told me you went in this direction to see if you could find the pilot and navigator. I just followed your footprints in the mud and snow." She looked down at Polina's still body. "Oh, no. Such a great person and pilot. We attended the same training classes." Galina looked over at the two dead German soldiers. "What happened here? How did you find them?"

"We were coming back from our last sortie of the night when their plane was hit. I saw them get hit by AA flak. If the German fighter planes had not come along and chased us, I could have landed right behind them. I circled around until I saw the flames from their plane and landed to see if they were alive. She can fill us in on the rest if you can help fly them back to our base."

"Of course, my plane was redesigned to carry wounded and passengers. I have a stretcher on my plane; we can carry Polina back on that.

But we must hurry. On my way down I saw a lot of German troop movement heading this way."

"Do not go by way of the open field," Katrina said. "It has landmines. I will stay here with my friend until you return."

Galina raced back to her plane, informed Ksenia what was going, and return to Vera and Katrina. They placed Polina's body on the stretcher and hurried through the trees to their planes. Quickly, they got Polina and Katrina into Galina's plane. They helped each other get the propellers started and flew off toward their base.

Polina was given a hero's burial and awarded the Hero of the Soviet Union posthumously. Katrina was also awarded the Hero of the Soviet Union medal. But it was a different Katrina who received the medal. She withdrew from attending any dances or parties and was very solemn. There was no laughter in her eyes, and none escaped her lips. She stayed in her quarters and didn't venture out except to go on sorties, the mess hall and base toilet.

A couple of months later, Vera and Ksenia tricked Katrina into coming with them, supposedly they needed to pick up supplies from the nearby town. However, there was a dance being held in town by the soldiers stationed there and that was really where they were planning on taking her.

A young, fresh-faced soldier in a jeep picked the three women up. It was prearranged by Vera and Ksenia and okayed by their base commander.

"What is this?" Katrina asked as the jeep pulled up to their quarters.

"Oh, we are going to have too many supplies to carry, so this soldier is taking us into town." Katrina was ushered into the front seat while Vera and Ksenia hopped into the back.

The ride was silent, even though Vera and Ksenia tried to pull the driver or Katrina into a conversation.

They arrived at one of the few buildings still left standing in the village. Already the sound of laughter and music could be heard drifting outside.

"Oh, it sounds like they are having a dance," Ksenia said excitedly.

"It will not hurt to go in for a couple of minutes," Vera spoke as if it were just a fluke they happened to be driving by the dance. "Come on you two. Let us go in and see what is going on."

"I will sit here," Katrina dropped her head and folded her hands on her lap.

"I will sit here with her. I do not feel much like dancing." He switched off the engine of the jeep.

"It is Comrade Corporal Georgie Spokva, is that not your name," Vera asked innocently. "Your brother was a pilot. He was shot down a couple of months ago. He was a true hero of the Soviet Union."

"Yes. Yes, he was," Georgie responded proudly.

"My best friend was a pilot, and she was killed," Katrina spoke quietly. "I am sorry to hear that your brother was killed. I am very sorry. I had two brothers killed at the front line; I know how you feel."

"It is such a helpless feeling. A feeling that hurts so deep you think it will never go away. I am sorry you lost your brothers and your best friend." He reached behind him and pulled out a woolen blanket. "Here this will keep you warm while they are inside dancing." Georgie flipped the blanket open and placed the large blanket over her lap.

"We can share it," Katrina said.

"Time for Comrade Ksenia and me to go." Vera patted Katrina on the shoulder.

Katrina opened her door as Vera and Ksenia climbed out of the jeep.

Georgie leaned around Katrina, pulled her door shut and began readjusting the blanket around them. As they walked away Vera and Ksenia heard Georgie say, "I do not mean to be disrespectful, but I have never seen such beautiful hair. Ever."

It was less than an hour before Georgie and Katrina came into the dance. Both were laughing and talking to each other, totally unaware of anyone else in the room. When a slow dance started, Vera watched as the two young people embraced. They stood together, more than danced, but Katrina looked happy for the first time in a long time.

* * *

Georgie and his jeep became a regular fixture at the base, and he always seemed to time his arrival exactly when Katrina would be around.

Vera went to Major Voskolov's base headquarters, and a half-hour later she walked out with a big smile on her face.

Ksenia was headed toward the mess hall when she saw Vera walking out of the captain's quarters. "What did you mess up this time?"

Vera laughed, "Nothing. In fact, I think I did a great job."

"Uh, huh? What great job?"

'I went in and asked that she transfer Katrina to be her assistant."

"No, you did not," Ksenia responded in shock.

"Yes. Yes, I did," Vera smiled and clapped her hands together.

"I think that is wonderful. I would so like her to live through this terrible war. That last flight of hers almost killed her and the pilot. I thought for sure they were not going to make it because their plane was so badly shot up. I truly have no idea how the pilot got it back to the base," Ksenia shook her head.

"I know. I thought her family had suffered so much, and so has Katrina. Her hands and knees were burnt, but luckily not severely. I kept thinking what about the next sortie. What if something worse happened to her? Anyway, I thought it was worth a try."

Ksenia slapped Vera on the back. "How did you do it?"

"At first the commander was hesitant because Katrina was a trained navigator, but I explained that she was excellent in details, knew all about the planes, schedules, flight crews, and would make a perfect assistant to her. And, Katrina was very good at finding out whatever needed to be found out."

"So, what did she say," Ksenia asked excitedly.

"I think she thought about it for about a split second and then agreed with me. Katrina is now her assistant, effective immediately."

Later that day Katrina came into their dugout, her face registered confusion. "Comrade Major Voskolov has reassigned me to be her assistant. Did I do something wrong? Why am I being pulled from my sorties? I am a trained navigator. How can I fight the fascists from a desk?"

Vera spoke up, "You did nothing wrong, Comrade Katrina, just the opposite. Captain Voskolov must think highly of you to ask you to be her assistant. That is a very high honor."

"Yes," Ksenia commented. "Your being familiar with the planes, navigation and attention to details is what she needs to help run this base at a higher level."

"You can fight the fascists by making sure everything is correct and accounted for." Vera hugged Katrina and kissed both of her cheeks. "Congratulations Comrade on your promotion."

"I have been promoted?" Katrina blinked her big, blue eyes in surprise.

"Of course. What did you think this was?' Ksenia hugged and kissed Katrina, too. "Congratulations, Comrade, from me as well. You will be able to tell Comrade Georgie tonight."

"Oh," Katrina's face lit up. "I will be able to see him a little more. So, this is not such a bad thing after all."

"No, Comrade, it is not such a bad thing after all," Vera stated. "But we must get ready to fly out tonight. And, we will feel safe knowing that you are looking after us down here."

"We will?" Ksenia mumbled.

"Shhh," Vera glanced back at Katrina, who luckily had not heard Ksenia's comment.

Chapter 11

Senior Major Voskolov called all the pilots and navigators to convene at base headquarters for a meeting. A map was spread out on the large wooden table. "We have been instructed to stop the enemy ferry from crossing the Terek River." She outlined with her finger where the enemy forces would be coming from. "You will commence the attack at 1800 hours."

Vera checked her watch. They had four hours before they were to fly out and stop the Germans. She sighed deeply. None of the pilots got any sleep that day. All of them had to fly during the day because the additional pilots had yet to arrive. So not only were they flying their eight to ten sorties a night, but during the day they had to drop off supplies, spies, papers, generals and important information to the front lines. No one seemed to care that they had not eaten all day, and flown all night dropping bombs on the enemy until early light. She was beyond exhaustion and hunger.

Vera entered her quarters grumbling with the rest of the pilots and navigators. Everyone hurried to their prospective plank beds and tried to get a few hours of sleep in before they had to fly out.

The fire in the oil drum heating their dugout was almost out. The air was frigid as Vera and the other women quickly threw branches gathered earlier into the oil drum. The wood hissed and spit, as the girls stumbled toward their beds. They fell on them hoping they could grab the couple of hours of sleep they so desperately wanted and needed.

Lieutenant Natalya Mykolina could not sleep: The anxiety, hunger, and the terror of dying were too great for her. She looked over at Vera, who had closed her eyes, but she could tell she was not sleeping either.

"Are you sleeping?" Natalya said softly to Vera.

"No, I wish I could sleep," Vera replied groggily.

"I cannot sleep either," another woman called out.

Soon all the women got up and sat on their makeshift beds.

"Alright," Natalya's face lit up. "We are very tired we cannot sleep so, let us do some poems."

Vera smiled at the vivacious, pretty girl. "You can make up such beautiful poems. Please, you start," she nodded for Natalya to begin.

Natalya sat for a moment in thought and then began her poem, and when she was finished there was total silence.

"You make us strong and proud," Vera said.

"We are sisters, are we not," Natalya smiled at the women in the damp, musty dugout.

Lt. Agrippina Makovich blew her nose on a scrap of material, "Thank you Natalya for always giving us something beautiful to think about. I am always afraid when I get into my plane that I will not return. But when you tell us one of your beautiful poems, I do not fear death. I almost embrace it. Your words always stay with me when I fly." Her straight, short, brown hair fell in front of her round, pale face. She was not a pretty girl, and her large hips made her look fat, which she was not.

"Do you have another poem to share," Vera asked. She knew Natalya loved to perform her poems.

Natalya stared at her close friends and comrades, "I would like to say a poem for my two children. I pray they are safe."

"Yes," Agrippina said. "I have a child who is now in the care of my mother. Please. Please give us another poem."

Natalya finished her poem as tears ran down her face, along with everyone else. "I say this poem with love to all of our children."

Vera shook her head, "I do not have any children, but your poem makes me feel I should go out and get one."

Everyone laughed, and the atmosphere in the room changed from being stressed beyond their endurance to embracing life and relaxing.

Natalya looked around the room at the red eyes of the women and smiled. "I have another," Natalya said. "Would you like to hear it?"

A resounding "yes" came from all the women.

Natalya finished her poem to the hearty laughter of all the women.

"You are a wonderful mistress of the poem," Vera said wiping a tear away that had rolled down her face from laughing so hard. "What did you do before the war broke out?"

"I was at the university studying to be an engineer," Natalya shrugged and then laughed. "My father and mother were both engineers, and they felt I should follow in their footsteps. Not so much was it my dream. I so longed to be a writer."

"You can write and be an engineer," Agrippina said. "It would be a very big crime for you not to be a writer, especially one that writes poems. I was in the university to become a scientist. I know I do not look too smart, but I really am."

Everyone laughed and soon they were talking about what they were studying at the university before they joined the women's army.

"We are kind of the elite. Like my navigator, Corporal Lubova Drukova. She was a great seamstress, but decided it was not enough and went to the university to become a psychologist," Agrippina said. "It appears that all pilots and navigators had been in the university."

"Yes. Yes, it does," Vera said. "I never paid too much attention to that fact before."

They sat and talked among themselves for the remainder of the four hours. All too soon they were called to start their sortie. Vera and Natalya walked together toward their planes. Their two navigators walked behind them talking and laughing.

"Thank you, Natalya, for giving us all a laugh and a good cry," Vera pulled her leather cap out of her pocket.

"I love these brave women. And, I love making up poems. If I can give them a moment of laughter or tears to take their minds off this horror we are living, then I gladly do it." Natalya reached her plane and turned to Vera. "Be safe and fly with God comrade."

"You as well, my friend." Vera said putting on her leather helmet. She reached her plane, took a deep breath and scrambled onto the wing of the plane and climbed into her cockpit.

Ksenia did a last-minute inspection of their plane and climbed in when the signal went out for the women to start their engines.

They were informed that the Germans had a heavily armed base set up across the Terek River, and the Soviet troops were on the bank on the other side. The women were to drop bombs on the German base and try to blow up their ammunition dump, and any boats that they planned on using to cross the river. They were told the most important target was their ammunition pile.

Darkness gave them a little advantage, but the Germans were used to the little Biplanes and the havoc they inflicted on their troops and supplies. All the women were aware of that as they headed for their new target.

Vera thought back on the time the base commander felt they should fly three abreast into the combat zone. Two would be decoys, and one would steal off in the darkness and drop her payload and then repeat everything until all three planes deployed their bombs. All though it was effective, the women incurred heavy losses, so it was decided that they would fly two abreast instead, using the same strategy, less one plane. Vera shivered from the cold air tugging at her cap, and the terror she felt each time they had a sortie. Flying two abreast was just as dangerous she thought, but it was ordered, and she had to follow orders.

The planes rumbled down the grassy landing strip and flew into the darkened sky. It was a clear, dark night as they approached their target two by two.

Vera's team flew in first. She pulled back on the throttle slowing the plane so that the engine sound would become softer. As she approached their target, the second plane veered off and headed directly over the base.

Immediately, search lights filled the sky. Tracer bullets from the anti-aircraft weapons began tearing through the inky blackness surrounding them.

The decoy plane weaved and flew erratically to keep the bright lights searching for it, as Vera flew into the darkness to drop her bombs. She gave the signal for Ksenia to drop their bombs. All seemed to be going as planned when Ksenia yelled in Vera's ear that one of the bombs was stuck.

Ksenia took off her gloves, and slowly climbed out on the wing of their plane. She braced herself with the metal wiring as she lay flat on the wing. On her belly, she inched her way to the edge and felt around for the strap that held the stuck bomb.

Bullets flew and zipped through the wing just missing her. Her fingers hurt from the cold as she frantically searched for the strap. Finally, she found it and grabbed the strap, yanking it sharply to release the bomb.

The concussion from the bomb exploding below jarred their plane, causing Ksenia to slip toward the end of the wing. A couple of anti-aircraft cannons exploded near their plane causing her to slide further off the wing. Ksenia frantically grabbed hold of the wire struts of the wing. Her fingers were beginning to numb from the freezing cold, as she hung half on and half off the wing.

Vera watched in horror as Ksenia struggled to get back on the wing. Vera quickly turned the plane on its side as rounds of flak smashed all around them. Her eyes were tearing up, and she could barely breathe, but Vera kept her attention focused on Ksenia.

With the plane tilted, Ksenia maneuvered herself back on top of the wing and slid toward the body of the plane. She reached up and grabbed the side of her cockpit and swung her leg over and fell more than crawled back inside.

Now with Ksenia safely inside, it was Vera's turn for them to become the decoy plane as she circled back around. She came in at a higher altitude, but it wasn't high enough to escape the machine-gun fire and the anti-aircraft cannons. Vera weaved in and out of the bright search lights.

The flak increased. Vera and Ksenia began choking and coughing and unable to breathe from the gun powder bursting around them. Then she heard the bombs exploding below and knew the second plane had dropped its payload. Vera pulled up hard and flew as fast as possible out of the sight of the searchlights. It took her eyes a while to adjust back to the dark from the glaring, brilliance.

Vera looked back and saw Natalya's plane dropping her payload and then circling around to take up position as the decoy. Vera headed her plane back to base to reload their bombs.

* * *

Natalya flew directly into the search lights trying to divert all the attention to her plane. They were jarred hard by a powerful burst of a shell and flak powder. It was difficult to breathe as she gasped for air. She looked over at her wing and saw flak had struck it causing one of the wings wires to snap. Natalya could not see the second plane from the constant glare of the bright lights below. She swerved, dodged and climbed to try to keep German gunners below focused on her plane. Then something went horribly wrong.

Natalya's eyes caught a burst of light from within the dark recesses where the search lights were not illuminating. It was the second plane of her team. She did not hear any explosion from the plane's payload dropping down on the enemy. Instead, the second plane had been hit and was on fire.

Natalya flew out of the glare from the search lights. It took her eyes a moment to adjust fully to the darkness now surrounding her. She screamed when she saw the second plane in her attack team blazing. It was Agrippina and Lubova's plane. Natalya's watched in horror as the injured plane headed straight for the ammunition dump. The Germans were throwing everything they could at the little plane, but Agrippina managed to steer it directly into their ammunitions pile.

The impact of Agrippina's plane into the ammunitions pile caused an explosion so strong Natalya's plane was blown sideways. Then, something struck Natalya's plane causing her to grab the throttle and hold it tightly. Suddenly, Natalya could no longer feel anything beneath her. She looked down, and the floor of her cockpit had been shot out from under her.

A small scream escaped from Natalya, as she felt the searing pain of shrapnel sticking out of her leg.

Natalya turned to see if her navigator, Corporal Darya Feskovo was alright, but she wasn't there. "Darya," she screamed, horrified that Darya's floor had been ripped out as well, and Darya was gone.

Natalya struggled to control the loosened throttle that was barely hanging on.

Her fuel line was hit. Suddenly, gas erupted spraying the small windshield and Natalya. Her eyes were burning from the fuel, and she was momentarily blinded. She knew one spark and the plane would burst into a blaze of fire.

Frantically, she looked around to see where she could safely land. Natalya's seat starred to wobble. She looked down and saw that the shrapnel had not only lodged in her leg, took out the floor of her cockpit, but had also dislodged her seat as well. If she didn't land the plane soon her seat would drop taking her with it. Disoriented by the spraying fuel and fumes, she started to become groggy. Her vision was blurred, and the fumes were making her dizzy. She knew she had to land and land fast.

Shaking her head to try to keep from passing out she grabbed for the smelling-salts, a small bottle of ammonia, but it had been hit and the bottle was empty. Natalya managed to find an updraft and rode it until she spotted an open field below. She prayed it was a Soviet-held field, because she was losing control of the plane fast.

The ground seemed to be miles below, but it was only a few feet. Natalya was losing perspective. She was dizzy and with every fiber in her body, she fought to stay alert. She pulled back on the throttle and landed hard on the ground. The plane bumped and jumped until it finally came to a stop.

Natalya climbed out onto the wing and looked into Darya's cockpit. She sighed with relief. Darya was slumped down in her seat; blood was running down her forehead, but she was alive. Suddenly, there was a burst of flames. Natalya frantically shook Darya.

"Darya quick the plane is going to explode," Natalya screamed.

Darya regained consciousness and quickly joined Natalya on the wing of their plane. She was still groggy from her head wound, but saw that Natalya had a serious leg injury. "Wait," she said and jumped to the ground to help her down. Darya put Natalya's arm around her shoulder, and the two women hurried from the burning plane as fast as they could.

The plane exploded throwing deadly shards and debris. Natalya screamed in pain as both women hit the ground to avoid flying pieces of the wreckage. Uninjured from any fragments from the plane the two women lay there unmoving. After a moment, Darya grabbed snow from the ground and held it to her gaping head wound. She grimaced in pain, "Maybe this will halt the blood flow a little."

"Come on," Darya said to Natalya. "We have to get moving. I do not know if we are behind enemy lines." She looked solemnly around her. Her leather cap was askew, and her brown hair was blowing wildly around her square-shaped face. Her gray-green eyes blinked furiously from the blood that kept trickling down her forehead into her eyes.

"I can make it, comrade." Natalya said. She turned onto her back and did not move for a moment. "Comrade listen to me. If we are in enemy territory, we cannot be captured. If we are, we must each shoot and kill the other, so we will not be tortured by the fascists."

"Agreed," Darya said.

"Okay, help me get up," Natalya reached her arms out for Darya to pull her to her feet.

But as Darya tried to pull her up, Natalya screamed in pain.

Darya dropped to her knees and gently eased Natalya to a sitting position. "You can do this," Darya said as she began to lift Natalya from behind.

Natalya bit her lip to keep from screaming anymore. "I have to stand up, or we will be caught."

"You are almost there," Darya said as she continued to lift Natalya.

Finally, Natalya could stand, but when Darya let her go; she began to fall again. "Darya, get me to that fallen log, so I can sit for a minute. I have a scarf that I can place over your head wound to try to stop the bleeding."

"No, you will need it for your wound. Let me see how badly you have been wounded." Darya helped Natalya to the fallen tree where she carefully inspected her wound. "I think the bullet missed your bone, but it made a nasty hole in your leg. Give me your woolen cap, I will make a tourniquet from your scarf." A few minutes later, Darya finished the tourniquet for Natalya's leg.

"Darya, I have an idea for your head wound. Quickly, take off your helmet, and your woolen cap." Natalya folded the woolen cap over the wound and had Darya put her leather helmet back on. "That should keep pressure on your wound until we can get help."

"We have to get moving." Darya carefully helped Natalya to her feet. "See whether this stick will help you walk better."

Natalya tried to walk a couple of steps with the large stick and smiled, "It helps a little. Thank you."

They supported each other by putting their arms around each other's waist. It was slow going as they headed away from the burning plane. Minutes turned into hours as they walked and stumbled through the uneven terrain.

"You have to rest." Darya's hold tightened around Natalya's waist.

"No," Natalya protested. "If I sit down, I know I will not be able to take another step."

A couple of minutes later, Natalya spotted a bridge off in a distance. "If we can make it to that bridge over there maybe we can catch one of our trucks or something."

"I am beyond cold," Darya said. "We have to get warm soon, or we will die from exposure."

"So you are saying we are not dead yet," Natalya said mockingly. "I thought we were."

"No. It just feels like we should be," Darya went to say something and stopped. "Shhh, I see movement by the bridge. I cannot make out if it is one of ours, or a fascist."

They didn't have to wait long to find out if it was friend or foe. Behind them, a male voice ordered them to stop. To their relief, it was a Russian voice.

"We are Soviet pilots and need help," Natalya said turning around to face the soldier. She saw more soldiers coming from the wooded area nearby.

"There is a military truck coming to drop off supplies. We will have them take you to the hospital right away." The soldiers quickly assisted both women to the bridge. Within minutes, a Soviet truck pulled up, and after it was unloaded, the two women were transported to the military hospital.

Chapter 12

Vera was ecstatic when she received her fifth letter from Yuri. They had kept in touch as much as they could over the last year, and every letter made her heart sing. He was busy with the wounded, and she was still doing extra duty flying during the day.

One day, she received orders to fly a general to the airfield where the 587th Women's Day Bomber Regiment was based. At this base, the women flew the bomber/fighter Petylakov's, or as everyone called them the PE-2's. Vera was somewhat familiar with them, although she had never seen one up close.

She preferred flying her little Biplane, even though sleep was becoming almost non-existent in her life. Twice she and Ksenia fell asleep at the same time. They came up with a plan that one would sleep going to the bombings and the other on the way back. Although she is quite certain from time to time they had both fallen asleep, again, at the same time, but luckily awoke in time to keep from crashing.

Vera landed in a field right off the make-shift runway for the PE-2's. Her passenger, the General, got out on the wing, jumped down and headed for the base command center without a word to Vera.

She raised her arms and stretched them as far as she could. "Feels good," she muttered. Vera sat in her plane for a couple of minutes and then climbed out and began walking around the PE-2's that were almost twice the size of her Biplane.

"Good morning," a woman's friendly voice said.

"Oh," Vera gasped a bit. "You startled me."

"Sorry," she said as her dark hair blew around her face. "I did not mean to startle you. I just saw you admiring my plane and thought I would say hello."

Vera saluted her and said, "Senior Captain Zhkov, pilot in the 588th."

"Senior Captain Sophie Cherkov, pilot of this beautiful PE-2." Her large brown eyes almost glowed as she talked about her plane.

"Sophie Cherkov?" Vera queried.

"Yes," Sophie said rather puzzled. "Yes, I am Sophie Cherkov."

"Oh, please excuse me; it is just I have heard your name mentioned several times by Senior Lieutenants Elena Petrovka and Oxana Jurvoika. Comrade Oxana said that you went through training with her. I was fortunate to have met her several times, and Elena was a very dear friend."

"Their deaths tore through me like fire," Sophie shook her head. "They were not only great human beings, but wonderful friends. I ache for them every day. They were here many times before their terrible deaths."

"It gripped my heart as well," Vera said sadly.

"Well, any friend of theirs is a friend of mine," Sophie leaned forward and kissed Vera on both cheeks. "Come I will show you this magnificent plane while they are refueling your plane."

"I would like that very much." Vera followed her around the front of the plane.

"Unlike your Biplane, we have protection." They climbed onto the wing, and Sophie's pretty, angular face came alive as she began to show Vera her plane. "As you can see this carries a three-woman crew. This is where I sit," she said pointing to the pilot's seat.

Vera held back her smile at the sight of two pillows on the pilot's seat.

"I see you noticed my pillows. I am not so tall," Sophie just shrugged. "The only complaint I have is that the control stick is so heavy. Sometimes my navigator helps when I am getting ready to take off by pushing on my back. Together we must push the stick to get the tail up, so

I can take off, unless I am very mad. Then I have great strength surge through me."

"I know that feeling. I have had great spurts of strength, and did not know where it came from," Vera replied.

"I agree," Sophie smiled. "In the Biplanes, the navigator sits behind you in her own cockpit. The navigator sits with me in the cockpit, but directly behind me. And our radio operator, who is also our gunner, sits down there." She opened the hatch so that Vera could peer in.

"There are two fixed guns that fire forward. And we have more fire power," she pointed to the acrylic bubble behind the navigator's seat, "that is where they house the swiveling machine gun. The navigator complains that the fumes are very strong in there, and sometimes she gets dizzy."

"That can be dangerous," Vera said admiring the well-armed plane.

"Yes, but she is aware of it, and she is not in there too long," she continued, "The radio operator can fire two more guns – see," she pointed to the two guns. "One gun fires from the floor just under the aircraft and the other machine gun fires through a hatch above her head."

"So, the radio operator has two guns to fire. I see boxes of spare ammunition belts for her guns all around her equipment."

"Oh, yes. And many times, she has run out of ammunition. We are supposed to be bombers, but we can be a fighter plane as well. This good old girl can move pretty fast."

"Maybe someday they will give us a machine gun to protect ourselves," Vera said as she moved back onto the wing of the plane.

"I do not understand why they have not yet done so." Sophie climbed out onto the wing of the plane next to Vera.

"We do not understand either," Vera jumped down to the frozen ground. "Thank you, Comrade, for the tour of your plane; I truly enjoyed seeing it."

Sophie nodded sadly, "I never thought I would be proud of a killing machine."

"None of us did," Vera said. "My brother was killed the first day the Fascists attacked our Motherland."

"I was away at the university. It was my first year. I remember laughing and having such fun with my fellow classmates. Life was good," she smiled, and then her eyes darkened. "My family lived in a small village near Kiev. They came through my village and," Sophie's voice began to crack.

Vera put her hand on Sophie's shoulder, "You do not have to go on."

Sophie reached up and patted her hand, "It is alright. It is their memory that keeps me fighting mad." She leaned back against the plane and continued. "They tortured my family before they shot them. All except my youngest sister and brother who hid from them. They murdered everyone else. I keep asking myself, why? Why? My parents were good and kind people who worked hard to feed their family, and to send me to the university. They had no weapons. They were no threat."

"War is an ugly monster that gives uglier monsters the ability to do unspeakable things," Vera's jaw tightened. "I am so sorry for your loss. What of your younger brother and sister? Where are they now?

"After the Germans left our village, they were found by our troops and sent to an orphanage until our relatives came and got them. They were taken deep into our Motherland near Siberia until after the war. The Germans will not get that far. Not with me flying up there."

Vera smiled and nodded as she adjusted the leather strap over her shoulder that held a large pouch.

"I have kept you from delivering your dispatch," Sophie said apologetically. "I am sorry. I got carried away for a moment. Anyway, I am just so proud of this little airplane and what it can do."

"Justifiably so," Vera patted the wing and smiled at Sophie. "But my 'dispatch' as you call it was just the general," she shrugged. "I carry my personal stuff in here in case we have to stay at a base overnight."

After an hour, the general appeared and signaled for Vera to get ready to fly.

Vera waited until the general was seated in her plane, "Comrade Sophie stay safe and may God go with you," she said softly so that the general could not hear her added religious acknowledgement.

"As with you, Comrade, may God keep you safe," Sophie responded equally as soft and winked at Vera. And, then very loudly she yelled to Vera, who was climbing into her cockpit. "Fly well for the Motherland."

Vera and the general returned the salute as Sophie stood solemnly watching their little Biplane take off and head into the open sky. It was a clear day, and Sophie hoped they would make it safely back to their base.

All the planes sat on the field ready to go, but a fog was closing in and Sophie knew they would not be going up tonight. She headed back to her quarters to finish writing letters to her family.

* * *

Sophie's mechanics, Corporal Zoya Rosno and Senior Sergeant Maria Aresko, walked onto the airfield for their turn to patrol. They each carried a rifle slung over their shoulder, and a pistol snapped securely on their duty belt.

"We are here." Maria said, as the two women they were relieving waved to them and headed to their quarters.

"I am glad this is the last watch for tonight," Zoya said to Maria.

"Yes," Maria adjusted the rifle strap over her shoulder. "And the last watch for a couple of days, until our turn comes up again." A few strands of her dark-brown hair were sticking out from under her leather helmet.

"Fix your hair," Zoya pointed to the strands of hair on Maria's face.

"I know. I put my headgear on too fast," Maria poked the loose hairs back under the helmet.

"Too fast! I put mine on so slow; I am not sure I am even here," Zoya yawned wide and looked around the airfield. "Two hours of guard duty and two hours off - all night long. Who thought of that anyway?"

"I am not sure about that, but it is what we signed up for," Maria said as her dark-brown eyes scanned the airfield.

"Did you know what you were getting into when you enlisted?" Zoya asked Maria.

"Does anyone at war know what they are getting into? No, I did not know. How about you?" Maria inquired.

"The training was quite fun," Zoya smiled as she reflected. "I danced and mingled with so many handsome men. I thought war was going to be fun."

"Fun?" Maria gasped. "War fun? What were you thinking?"

"Obviously, not too clearly," Zoya looked up and down the airfield. "Then the fun was replaced with all the ugly things war brings. It was a hard reality call for me. War is so senseless."

"Yes, it is." Maria shook her head and began walking down the airfield.

Zoya kept pace with her long-legged friend, "But I must say I eat better. I have four brothers and five sisters, and we were lucky if we ate once a day. There were days and days of just a thin broth of old cabbage soup. Here I get three meals a day."

"We get very little sleep," Maria yawned.

"My family lived in an apartment with one bedroom," Zoya laughed. "There was constant chaos, so I know what having no sleep is about. I almost looked forward to going to work in the factory. It was quieter there."

"I worked in a factory, too. I had a large family living in a tiny apartment. So I can relate to everything you have just said," Maria shook her head and smiled. "I just wish there was peace."

"Yeah, me, too. But right now, I am so tired I can barely see," Zoya yawned again. "And, besides that, I do not like standing guard here," Zoya pouted. She scrunched up her face. Her small, green eyes squinted against the cold wind. "I get frightened by all the strange noises coming from the woods over there."

"You never mentioned that before. What strange noises?" Maria asked looking down at her partner.

"Umm, I hear howling and sometimes I see movement in there," Zoya replied nervously.

"How strange you would hear 'howling' in a forest," Maria said sarcastically. "Ah, I know what is lurking in the forest, it is Baba Yaga.

Her house may be close by." Maria turned her head so that Zoya could not see the grin spreading across her face.

"Baba Yaga?" Zoya almost screamed the name. "Is Baba Yaga a real person, I mean witch? I thought she was just a scary story my brothers used to tease me about. I am nineteen. Baba Yaga only goes after little children."

Maria turned to Zoya; her face very serious. "I am only twenty and I would still be afraid of Baba Yaga. Age does not matter to her. You did not know this?"

Zoya shook her head. Her brows furrowed, and her eyes narrowed, as she looked at the line of trees across the field.

"I bet her house is somewhere close by. One minute you can see her and the next she disappears. And, the scariest thing is she can change into any shape."

Zoya just stood there her eyes widened, as she stared at the trees off in the distance.

"Zoya?" Maria called her name, but Zoya kept staring across the open field to the forest. "Zoya! I was joking," Maria rolled her eyes.

"I knew that," Zoya said, although her voice displayed a slight quiver to it. "I knew that," she repeated nervously. "I knew all along you were joking."

"Well, I wish she was real. Maybe she would destroy the fascists running around in our forests." Maria snorted.

"I am cold, hungry and tired," Zoya gave her best pout. "Why do we have to patrol, especially at nighttime?"

"Because there is no one else to patrol, but the ground crews. And why do we have to patrol? Because if we do not, we will be shot," Maria said slightly annoyed with Zoya. She pulled the collar of her coat up around the bottom of her ears. "You are a very short woman," she said gazing down at Zoya.

"No," Zoya huffed to her friend who towered over her. "You are just a very tall woman. What are you seven feet tall?"

"No, six foot two," Maria's teeth chattered a bit as she spoke.

"Like I said, seven feet tall." Zoya placed her rifle on the wing of a plane. She crossed her arms and began rubbing them gently to get heat to them. "If I hear or see someone, I think I would faint first and shoot later," Zoya picked up her rifle from the top of the wing. "And if you find me flat on my face in the snow, step over me; I am just sleeping."

"We will have plenty of time to sleep when the war is over." Maria adjusted the rifle over her shoulder. "We must patrol now. I will head back that way." She pointed toward the farthest end of the airfield where everyone's quarters were situated.

"Wait," Zoya said in alarm. "I will be walking nearest the forest?"

"Yes," Maria raised the palms of her hands. "What is the problem?"

"Well, I never worried about walking patrol on that side before, until you had to mention Baba Yaga. I had forgotten all about her." Zoya looked at Maria, back at the forest line, and back at Maria again.

"Comrade Zoya, the forest is so far away that if you see Baba Yaga coming just call out, and I will come running. I will have more than enough time to get here." Maria bit her lip to keep from laughing.

"All right," Zoya tried and failed to give a sincere smile. "I will walk around the planes that way, and we will meet back here. The walking may warm us up."

Zoya reached the end of the field and was about to turn around and head back when she saw a figure standing at the edge of the forest. She blinked a couple of times to make sure she really saw something, and then it was gone. She turned to call out to Maria when the figure appeared again. The figure kept walking toward her, and then it would disappear and suddenly reappear. "Stop who goes there?"

There was no answer. She gulped. "Baba Yaga? No, do not be silly, Zoya," she said. Then very loudly she yelled, "Stop! Who goes there? Please answer because I do not wish to shoot you. Please say something."

The figure still did not answer and kept coming closer. "I do not want to shoot you. Say something. Anything." Zoya called pleading with the figure to answer. She raised her rifle and shot in the air.

Maria heard the shot and raced back to where Zoya was standing. She looked down the field toward the forest and saw nothing. "What are you doing?" She yelled to a wide-eyed Zoya.

The gun shot woke up the base, and everyone was running, with their guns drawn, toward the two women standing at the end of the airfield.

Maria turned around in horror as she saw them coming toward them, "You just got us killed. They are going to shoot us for firing a gun at nothing."

The base commander reached the two women; his face flushed and angry. "Who fired that shot?"

"I did. There is someone out there, Comrade Commander," Zoya's voice broke into little gulps.

The commander stared intently at Zoya, and without taking his eyes off her, he called out loudly, "Who goes there?"

"Do not shoot." A male's voice called from a distance.

"Huh?" Maria's eyes grew wide as she slowly turned her head at the sound of the man's voice.

"I have an urgent message for the base commander," the deep male voice said.

"Go and get him," the commander ordered Zoya and Maria.

Both women ran to the prone figure and when they reached him; they saw the Russian uniform. "What is the matter with you?" Zoya yelled. "I could have shot you. Why did not you speak to me?" She asked angrily.

He looked up at the two women aiming their rifles at him and said, "I forgot the password."

"You were there. Then you were not. What kind of game were you playing?" Zoya questioned.

"No game," he said matter of fact. "It is icy and there are very big holes. I kept slipping and falling. Can I get up now?" He asked.

Maria nodded, but kept a watchful eye on him.

"I have to report to the officer in charge, which way is it?"

They led him to their commander, and after verifying that he was indeed a Russian soldier and not a spy, everyone hurried back to their quarters.

"Good work, comrades," the commander said. He left with the messenger and headed for the command center.

"Well, that got my body heated up very nicely." Zoya pulled her now too warm jacket out slightly from her body.

"Let us hope it will keep us warm for the next hour or so," Maria chortled. "Look, the sun has finally decided it has had too much sleep."

"Lucky for the sun," Zoya rested her rifle against her leg and stretched her arms. "Come on, we should check everything we did last night and make sure it is correct and secured." She picked up her rifle and headed for Sophie's plane.

Suddenly, Maria stopped, "Shhh," she quickly removed her head gear.

"What are you doing?" Zoya said aghast. "Your ears will freeze off."

"Do you hear that?" Maria scanned the skies.

Then Zoya heard the faint sound of airplanes heading toward the field, and it wasn't one of theirs. "Enemy aircraft." Zoya screamed to Maria.

"Sound the alarm," Maria yelled to Zoya as they began running back to the living quarters screaming, "German fighters. We are under attack."

Zoya raced to the old rusted siren and began winding its lever. The scream and wail of the siren brought everyone out of their quarters. The pilots, navigators and radio operators raced out carrying their duty belts in one hand and their headgear in another. They raced toward their planes falling to the ground as the Germans machine guns made a sweep of their field.

The three enemy fighters strafed the field and made a wide circle returning with their guns raging over the airfield. Two grounded planes caught on fire, and another plane exploded.

Sophie and her crew were on the other side of the field from where the explosion occurred and hurried to their plane. Only three crews were able to make that small window of opportunity to climb into their planes and try to get up in the air.

The planes were staggered so that they were not all sitting in a row, which made it harder for the German fighters to take out all their planes at the same time.

The Germans came back for another run, and their machine guns took out two more planes. One of the planes had all three of their flight crew inside the plane; the other plane was empty.

Unmindful of the machine-gun fire from the enemy planes, Zoya, Maria and the other mechanics stayed on the field firing their rifles and handguns as the enemy planes passed over them. One of the German planes took a direct hit from the bullets pouring out of their rifles and firearms. A black plume of smoke rose from behind the Messerschmitt as it plummeted into a copse of trees. The women didn't have time to celebrate as the remaining German fighters were circling again to make another attack.

Two fighter PE-2's got off the ground and climbed into the cloudy, morning sky. The German fighters stopped strafing the airfield and diverted their attention to the two fighter planes that had managed to get airborne. One enemy fighter zeroed in on the second Soviet plane in the air. The other Messerschmitt went after Sophie's plane. Bullets ripped into her plane, but no one inside was hit. Angered, Sophie pushed the throttle to full power. She slammed the stick to the right and rolled out of the line of fire of the Messerschmitt coming up behind her.

The German pilot flew past Sophie's plane so close she could have almost reached out and touched it. She saw the startled look on the pilot's face when he saw a woman piloting the fighter plane. Sophie didn't have time to put her leather headgear on, and her short brown hair fell in curls down to her shoulders. She saw him break into a huge grin as he broke away from Sophie's plane coming in behind her again.

"He turned and is coming in from the rear," the radio operator yelled up to her. Their communication system was knocked out at the first strike.

"You think shooting down women is easy, huh? Not this woman!" Sophie growled. "Hold on," she screamed back to the navigator and radio operator.

The German pilot caught up with Sophie's plane and shadowed her every move. He lined up for a kill when suddenly Sophie jammed her ruder down causing her plane to drop. It brought her up directly behind the enemy fighter. She lined her plane up for the attack. "Fire," she screamed.

She didn't have to tell the women to fire. They fired with everything they had and got a direct hit. A dark column of smoke rose out of the rear of the enemy fighter as it plummeted to the ground where it exploded on impact.

Now Sophie's attention was on the last German fighter that had been attacking the other Soviet plane. A short moment later, the German pilot stopped his assault and flew away. At first, Sophie was surprised, and then saw three more of their PE-2 fighter planes had joined them. The German fighter was vastly outnumbered and had made a run for it.

The pilots checked out the skies before they returned to their airfield. They were greeted with cheers from everyone on the ground as they rolled into their space to park their planes.

"It was a good thing your planes were off the ground and patrolling the area," the commander said.

"We started running low on fuel and headed back to base to refuel," one of the pilots spoke with anger filling his voice. "I just wish we were here sooner."

"Fuel up and check the skies again," the commander ordered. He saluted the three pilots as they hurried toward their planes.

Sophie was horribly saddened by the death of three of her comrades. They had just gotten into their plane when it was hit by the enemy fighters. Two other people were seriously hurt on the ground, and the base was destroyed.

The base commander was giving orders to dismantle what they could. They had to find another airfield because the Germans were now aware of this base and how to find it.

"See if you can fix the radio communications on our plane." She spoke directly to Zoya and Maria. "By the way, that was great work. You warned us just in time. And, I am not sure who shot the fascist plane down but thank you. I need my plane ready for take-off as quickly as possible. I have to scout for a new location for our base."

"Oh, wonderful," Zoya said sarcastically, as Sophie walked away. "We get to relocate – again."

Chapter 13

Vera was flying her ninth and last bombing sortie for the night and landed safely on the airfield. The sun was starting to rise, and the black edge of night gave way to the misty rays of another day.

As Vera stepped out of her plane, Rimma advised her that the base commander requested her presence immediately.

Tired from bombing for ten straight hours Vera shrugged and headed to the command dugout. Inside, the base commander was sitting around a wooden, plank table and another uniformed officer was sitting next to him. She saluted her superior officer and the general sitting next to him. "Comrade Senior Major Korkavic. Comrade Senior Captain Vera Zhkov reporting as requested." The major returned a formal salute, but the general looked the other way, with no return salute.

"You are to take Comrade General Hrtova to one of our bases at the front lines." He motioned for her to come closer and showed her on the map where he was to be taken.

"Can she read this map?" General Hrtova said sarcastically.

"She is one of my best pilots," Major Korkavic's blue eyes narrowed. "She can read any map and is noted for her great flying skills."

"She had better be the best," he snarled. "I am putting my life in the hands of a woman," he almost spat out the words 'woman.' "I am only letting her fly me to the front lines because I was informed you cannot," he said to the major. "Is her plane ready for takeoff?" He was ignoring Vera as if she wasn't even in the room.

"I sustained a few hits, and my mechanics are repairing and fixing any problems that may have happened during our last sortie, Comrade Sr. Major Korkavic." Vera looked past the general and spoke directly to the major.

"All women mechanics I assume," the general said disgustedly as he adjusted his black-rimmed glasses that had slid down his nose. "I cannot believe this is happening to me. All women. How deplorable is that?"

"I think you will find these women are just as good as any of the men mechanics and pilots you have encountered," the major said respectfully, but Vera could see his jaw tightening.

"Yes, Comrade Sr. Major, sir. We are as good as the men, because it was men who trained us," Vera averted her eyes from the glaring eyes of the general.

"Maybe women cannot comprehend what the men are training them," the general snapped.

Vera detested the balding general with his pinched face and beady eyes.

"Respectfully, Comrade General Hrtova, that may be in some cases, but not theirs." The major folded the map and handed it back to the general. "I will have some coffee brought to you while the mechanics make the necessary repairs for your safe flight." He got up and motioned for Vera to follow him. When they were safely out of hearing from the general, he turned to Vera. "I am sorry for his inexcusable arrogance."

Vera smiled at her new commander. He was assigned to their regiment after Senior Major Voskolov was tragically killed in a plane crash. The women were resentful at first when they heard a male was going to replace their beloved captain. However, the major proved to be a kind and fair commander. He was tall and extremely handsome and became an immediate heartthrob to most of the women.

"Thank you, Comrade Major Korkavic, but you never have to apologize to me for someone else's poor manners and judgments. We are proud to serve under your command."

The captain shuffled his foot in embarrassment, "Ahem, thank you, and I will say that I am proud to be in command of one of the finest units in this army – even though it is all women." They both laughed and headed for the poorly constructed mess center.

"Get a quick bite of something, and some coffee to keep you going for a while. If you can grab a couple of minutes of sleep before you have to fly out that is even better." He reached over and touched her arm, "And that is an order."

Vera knew she did not have time to take a nap; instead, she went to the mess hall.

Ulyana was there as usual with her winning, child-like smile. "I will get you a good, hot cup of coffee and some bread and a little sugar, maybe." She hurried to the counter and poured coffee and sliced some bread and brought it to Vera with almost a skip in her step.

"How are you doing, Comrade Ulyana?" Vera asked as she sipped a hot cup of coffee.

"I am doing quite well, thank you, Comrade Sr. Captain Vera," she said. "I am helping my Motherland, by helping those who are fighting. And, I have made many new friends." She waved at the two young women in the kitchen, who smiled and waved back at her. "I must go and help prepare for the afternoon meal. Good-bye Comrade Sr. Captain Vera."

Vera nodded and smiled. While she finished her coffee, with a little sugar in it, and her bread, she studied the location on the map where she was to deposit the general. She was familiar with the location and was looking forward to getting rid of the nasty, arrogant general as fast as she could.

It was just over an hour before her plane was patched, refueled and ready to fly.

"Our men ground crews would have had this plane ready an hour ago," the general grumbled.

"Comrade General, please be sure to buckle up. The air currents can get very bumpy at times." Vera said respectfully.

The general pushed her aside as he pulled his long, thin frame up on the wing and then climbed into the navigator's cockpit.

Vera looked at Rimma and Larissa's shocked faces. She just winked, gave a small smile and nodded for them to start her propeller as she climbed into her cockpit.

Rimma flipped the propeller around, but the engine did not turn over. She attempted again and still the engine did not start.

From behind Vera heard the disgruntled general's disgusted sighs. Finally, there was ignition and the engine began to purr. After Rimma was a safe distance away from the whirling propeller blades, Vera headed down the bumpy, lumpy field.

Soon her plane was soaring into the clear blue sky, and the ride became smoother. There was no heat in the airplane and with open cockpits to the elements, their ride became much colder. Vera turned her head and saw the general grabbing his coat and gathering the front of it to try to get warm.

Their flight was uneventful until Vera spotted a small speck flying in the sky. It was far enough away that if it was an enemy plane, she hoped it would not see them. However, the speck became larger as her plane flew directly toward them. It was a free hunter Messerschmitt, and he had spotted them.

When it got within range, the German fighter opened fire at their plane. Vera pulled the throttle back as the bullets zinged and pinged around them. But neither pilot nor passenger was hit.

The enemy pilot flew around and came in behind their plane. Vera waited until the right moment and then broke a hard left. The Messerschmitt flew past her again with its bullets striking the open, empty air.

The Messerschmitt circled for another strike when Vera spotted a forest below her. As the pilot came in for a frontal attack, Vera dove straight down toward the trees below. The German fighter missed them again.

Vera could hear the general screaming like a little girl in the rear cockpit; she would have laughed, but she had to keep focused on the danger at hand.

Now Vera had somewhat of an advantage. She flew her plane in, and around the trees with ease banking left and right to avoid hitting the trees themselves. She glanced back for a second at the general. He was sitting there with his eyes fixed in terror, his mouth open and clutching his briefcase to his chest.

Carefully easing her plane back into the sky, Vera's head swiveled back and forth looking for any sign of the enemy's plane. The sky was clear. The enemy gave up, or ran out of gas; Vera didn't care, because either way it was gone. Quickly, Vera got back on course and flew the general to his destination without any further incidents.

She landed in an open field near the base and almost before the plane came to a stop the general climbed out on the wing, and as he went to jump to the ground, his legs gave out underneath him. Vera jumped down and extended her hand to help him up. He brushed it away, stood up by himself, glared at her and walked shakily away.

One of the male ground mechanics took one look at the general struggling to walk without shaking and began to laugh, "He looks like he saw a ghost. It appears you gave that general quite a great ride."

"Yes," Vera laughed. "I do not think he will forget that ride for a long time."

"We will get you fueled up so you can leave right away," he smiled. "Just in case he decides he wants you to fly him somewhere else."

"Oh my," Vera said. "Let me help you refuel it."

The mechanics finished refueling her plane and gave Vera the all clear signal. She climbed onto the wing and looked back at the mechanic. "This is probably the one and only time I am glad we do not have any radio communications. No one can order me to turn around and give him another ride." She climbed into the cockpit and put on her fur-lined leather cap and gloves.

"From the look on his face and his staggering walk, I do not think you have to worry about him wanting another ride with you, Comrade Senior Captain. Be safe." He walked to the front of the plane and wound the propellers.

The engine started, and Vera headed down the airfield and into the clear blue sky, and even though it was bitter cold, she relished flying the plane in the crisp, fresh air. After a while, she began to smell petrol. At first, it was just the faint smell of the fuel, and she attributed that to helping the mechanics wheel the petrol barrels and filling the tank. But now it was very strong. Unexpectedly, the petrol began to spray into her cockpit getting on her clothes and into her eyes.

Temporarily blinded by the spraying petrol Vera pulled the scarf around her neck to wipe it from her eyes and face. She had flown too far from the base where she had dropped off the general, and knew she was too far from her own base.

The plane started to choke and sputter. Vera's eyes were burning, and her vision wasn't clear. Blinking fast and hard, she managed to see a road below. It was a dangerous place to land, not knowing if it was in enemy territory. But she had no choice. She had to land the plane immediately.

She glided over the treetops as she struggled with the throttle to keep from hitting them. She pushed the throttle up to keep the plane from landing nose first.

The plane bounced and jerked when it hit the road causing a spark to ignite in the engine and the petrol in her cabin to erupt in fire. Vera scrambled out of the plane. Her clothes were on fire as she jumped from the moving plane into the snow.

Rolling in the snow, Vera managed to extinguish the flames, and pulled her scorched gloves off. She tried to get her burnt jacket and leather cap off, but her hands were too badly burnt. Then she heard a loud explosion and turned to see her plane burst into flames.

Not knowing where she was, or if she was in enemy territory, Vera started to stand up and screamed in pain. One of her legs had been injured when she jumped from the moving plane. She lay there not knowing what to do when she heard a sound that sent chills down her spine. It was the fascists. She tried desperately to retrieve her gun. Vera knew what the rules were. She had to kill herself. But her hands were so badly burnt she couldn't even feel the gun's holster.

The soldiers raced toward her, screaming in German. She only understood one word, Nachthexen: Night Witch. One of the soldiers was ordering her to do something, but she didn't understand anything he was saying. He grabbed her roughly by the collar and yanked her up. Vera screamed and fell to the ground grabbing her injured leg. Another soldier kicked her in the back, grabbed her collar and with the aid of another soldier, they dragged her across the field to a waiting truck.

As they pulled her across the rough terrain, Vera saw a couple of burned-out German tanks sitting on a steep hill, and all around the tanks lay the dead bodies of Soviet and German soldiers.

When the two soldiers got to the truck, they picked up Vera's body and slung her into the back of it. The pain was so excruciating, Vera blackout. When she awoke, she was freezing and in pain on a cold damp floor. Groggily, she looked around the room. It was completely bare. There were four stone walls, a very small window and a wooden door that cut through the gray stones.

A while later, the door to her cell opened, and a German SS officer walked in. He walked around her for a moment and began to speak to her in perfect Russian. "I see you are awake. I am the commander of this base, and I can make your life easy or difficult. Just tell me where the Soviet bases are located, and I will see that you are cared for immediately."

Vera just stared at him not saying anything.

"Come, come," he smiled falsely. "You must be in a great deal of pain. Look at your poor burnt hands. Even your arms and neck have nasty burns. Then there is your broken leg. Such a pity to be in such pain."

Vera still said nothing as terror, anger and hatred consumed her.

The officer moved closer to her and softly nudged her broken leg. "If you do not tell me we shall have your other leg broken as well," he shrugged and smiled coyly. "It is up to you."

Vera turned her head away from him. She had heard the horror stories of what the Germans did to their prisoners, especially female pilots. She bit her lip trying not to show fear.

The German officer began to raise his voice, "You will talk eventually. Trust me, you will." And with that he kicked her broken leg causing Vera to scream in pain. "You will get no food or water until you are ready to talk." He turned, looked down at the burns on Vera's hands and ground his foot on one of her hands. Vera shrieked in pain. "Next time will be worse." He snarled and walked out of her cell leaving her there in pain.

Two days went by, and he visited her everyday inflicting pain trying to get her to talk.

The third day the door to her cell opened, she closed her eyes and waited for the torture to begin. Instead, she felt gentle hands raising her head and someone pressing a cup to her lips. "My dearest, Vera."

Vera thought she was hallucinating. The voice seemed familiar. Then she felt water being poured into her mouth. She opened her mouth and greedily drank what was offered. She was afraid to open her eyes for fear it was just a dream.

"Vera," the voice said quietly. "Vera open your eyes."

When she opened her eyes, she was looking into Yuri's eyes. "Yuri? Is it really you?"

"I have gotten some medicine for your burns, and I must set your leg immediately. I have stolen some pain medicine and ointment for your burns. I must clean these burn wounds quickly." He picked up one of her hands and gasped. "What have they done to you?" He almost cried in shock.

"How did you get here?" She asked and let out a slight cry as he tried to clean her burns.

"I am sorry for the pain, but I must get these cleaned. Our base was captured and because I am a doctor, they let me treat not only their soldiers, but some of the wounded brought in that are ours."

"How did you get to see me?" She asked between gulps of water he was giving her.

"I speak German and understand it very well. But they do not know that. Only the young guard, Michael, standing there knows that. He befriended me and has helped with getting food and water to those he could."

"A fascist would do this?" Vera asked stunned.

"Remember it is the leaders who cause all the wars and some of the soldiers are forced into something they have no use for – probably on both sides. Michael is a poet of all things. He detests war, suffering, and killing on any level."

"How did you get that horrible commander to let you see me?"

"I saved the commander's wife when she was in labor. I delivered him a healthy son and made his wife well again. So, when I heard that a Soviet woman pilot was being held prisoner I asked to come here and care for her. For three days, I pleaded and finally went to his wife and pleaded with her. She intervened, and I got permission to visit the hated Soviet pilot woman. I had no idea it was you. Michael told me the woman had bad burns, and he thought a broken leg, so I came prepared. At least, I thought I was prepared. When I saw it was you, I thought my heart would stop."

"Has it been only three days? I feel like I have been here an eternity. I have told him nothing and will tell him nothing even if it means my death," she said adamantly.

"I know, my dear Vera. I know," he said gently stroking her cheek.

He heard Michael clear his throat, which was the signal that he must go. "I have brought you some bread. I will hide it under your arm. Try not to let them see you eat it. I was told I could only bring you water. Quickly, drink quickly." He reached behind her and helped her sit.

Vera drank the water as fast as she could gulp down and relishing every drop.

"I can leave this water here; it is not much, but I will get back to see you as often as I can," Yuri said as he stood up to leave. "By the way, Michael took your medals and Party membership card and hid them in your boot. He said when they first brought you in, you were thrown in here like a sack of potatoes. Your jacket was badly burned, and no one saw or paid any attention to the burnt medals. He said your oversized boot was the safest place to put them, because they were so badly burned no one wanted your boots."

"I do not understand why he did that," Vera's brows furrowed.

"He was afraid they would shoot you immediately if they found all your medals. He had never seen a woman pilot before and found you quite lovely," Yuri said. "I must go now." He walked to the cell door and looked back at Vera and smiled as he left her alone on the floor.

Vera wanted to call out and beg him to stay, but she knew he could not. The door to her cell slammed shut and for a moment she thought she had dreamed the whole thing, until she reached under her arm and found the bread there. Even though her hands still caused her pain, she grabbed the bread and began eating the stale bread as if it were the best thing she had ever eaten.

She awoke the next day to a strange quiet all around her. The light from the window faded into night and to her relief, the German SS officer did not make his daily visit to her. But neither did Yuri.

Another night and day of silence went by. Her bread and water had been gone for two days, and her thirst was over-powering.

Suddenly, a loud explosion outside of her cell caused pieces of the ceiling to fall on her. The air was filled with sounds of heavy artillery booming all around her, followed by machine gun and rifle fire.

Vera's cell door burst open and to her delight, it was a Soviet soldier. Vera sighed with relief. Her ordeal was over. Now she could heal and rejoin her regiment.

Chapter 14

The Soviet soldiers came into her cell and gently picked her up and took Vera outside into the sun light. She squinted hard against the brightness of it, while at the same time basking in its small warmth. The soldiers helped her to a bench where they told her that she was being transferred to a hospital as soon as the trucks got there.

Soon an officer and three soldiers carrying submachine guns walked over to her. "Who are you? Present your papers," he ordered rather severely; she thought.

"My boot, please, take off my boot," Vera raised her hands to show the burns and gestured toward her uninjured leg where her medals and papers were stashed.

The officer nodded toward one of the soldiers to take her boot off.

The soldier handed his submachine gun to one of the other soldiers, reached down and pulled off her boot. As soon as it came off her medals and identification papers fell to the ground. The soldier picked them up and handed them to the officer.

He looked them over, and his eyes hardened as he looked at Vera. "You have been here for many days. You must be very hungry." His voice was not friendly, and she detected a suspicious tone to it.

The officer whispered something to the three soldiers. Immediately, the two soldiers slung their weapons over their shoulders, reached down and roughly grabbed Vera. Holding her under each arm, they walked her toward a truck. She hobbled as fast as she could with each step bringing her severe pain.

When they got to the truck, they pushed her in. The soldiers were ordered to take Vera to the counter-espionage section of their division. She was put into a cell alone, with only a trestle bed. After a while, the cell door opened, and she was brought a bowl of broth which she greedily drank down. She had just finished the tasteless, but still welcomed broth, when the door opened and two armed guards told her to follow them.

They did not assist her up the flight of steps. Vera groaned with each step, but the soldiers paid no attention to her pain. When the pain would be too much she would stop on a stair, only to be pushed in the back by a rifle to keep moving from the soldier following behind her.

Vera was brought to a room that was sparsely furnished. There was an officer sitting behind a desk who motioned for her to enter. The door was left open, and the two soldiers stood outside of the door. A chair was in front of the officer's desk, and Vera ambled toward it when the officer shouted, "You do not have permission to sit."

Vera was stunned but stood at attention trying not to weave back and forth.

"How did you come by these papers?" He demanded as his steely-eyes peered up at her from behind a pair of wire-rimmed glasses. A bushy, reddish-colored mustache hung over his thin lips. The single light bulb above reflected on his bald head.

"Those are my papers and medals, Comrade Colonel," Vera said startled by his questions. "May I sit, Comrade Colonel?"

He ignored her request as he examined her papers and medals. After he scanned her papers over and over, he gestured for her to sit down.

Vera collapsed into the chair and sighed with relief until the colonel screamed at her, "Stand at attention!"

She struggled to her feet wavering from weakness.

"Where did you steal those decorations?" He pointed to her medals and papers sitting on his desk.

"They are mine Comrade Colonel," Vera said weakly.

"What was your mission? Who is your contact?" He demanded.

"My mission was to fly my PO-2…"

The colonel interrupted her before she could finish. He slammed his fist on the table and leaned menacingly toward her, "Stop lying you filthy, fascist whore! Who assigned you this mission to try to infiltrate our division? Is that why you were imprisoned inside of a German camp; you were posing as a prisoner so that you could infiltrate our Army?"

"Those are my papers and medals," Vera spoke quickly.

"Shut up, you lying, fascist spy," his lip curled and spittle sprayed from his mouth. He got up from behind his desk and walked around Vera as she weaved back and forth.

After hours of being interrogated by her own Soviet army, she was led away by two soldiers. The soldiers did not help her as she weakly climbed back down the stairs and when they opened her cell door, they roughly shoved her in.

The next day she was forced to walk up the steep steps again to the colonel's office and ordered to stand for hours while he interrogated her. He would shout at her, belittle her and even grabbed her burnt hands saying she would suffer even more if she did not confess that she was an enemy spy.

For four days, Vera endured the brutal, verbal assaults and the rough treatment from the soldiers. Each day she was brought one bowl of thick broth, and led to the bathroom once a day. The soldiers never locked her cell door, and the only words they spoke to her contained some of the foulest words she had ever heard.

Finally, on the fourth day of confinement, Vera cracked open the door to her basement cell; she saw that the soldiers were at the opposite end of the hall. She burst through the door and walked up the steep steps to the first floor.

The two soldiers on duty yelled for her to stop, or they would shoot her. She kept going until she got to the colonel's door. She thrust it open and began screaming. "You will not treat me like this anymore. Do you hear me? I am a PO-2 pilot in the Red Army, and all of those medals and papers are mine." Vera screamed at the surprised colonel behind his desk.

Two soldiers raced into his room with their guns drawn. "It is all right," the colonel said to the two stunned soldiers. "Leave the room." He ordered.

Confused, the two soldiers left the room and waited outside of his office.

"Sit down. Would you like a glass of water?" The colonel poured water in a glass and brought it to Vera.

Vera's hands were shaking so badly she could barely hold the glass to her lips. She drank the water, almost in one gulp, as it spilt down the front of her dirty and burnt tunic. She wiped her mouth with the back of her hand and fell more than sat on the chair in front of the colonel's desk.

"Well, I can see you are much calmer now," the colonel took the glass from her and walked back to his desk and sat down. "I have many, many papers requesting your release from an army doctor; a Doctor Yuri Dreklin and many others. He took great pains in trying to find out where you were. When he was informed you were being tried for being a spy, he explained how you were captured, and your horrible treatment by the fascist pigs."

Vera bit her tongue for fear she would say something to the colonel about his treatment of her that could get her shot.

"He was a very busy man. He contacted many influential people, and he has attested, with many others, that you are, in fact, who you say you are." He shuffled a couple of papers on his desk and then looked at her. "I found it strange that you had managed to preserve all of your identification in such a horrible confinement. When Comrade Doctor Dreklin tried to explain that a German fascist had put your information into one of your boots. Well, that led us to believe that he did not realize you could probably be a fascist spy. After all, why would a German fascist help the enemy? I had to make sure for our Motherland. I am sure you understand."

"I would like to return to my regiment," Vera said icily.

"Your good friend, the doctor, has not left town. So, I had him informed that you were going to be released today. He has arranged to have a truck brought, and you are to be taken to a military hospital to have your wounds taken care of properly."

Vera bit her lip to stop from crying. Finally, it was over. She was going to be treated for her wounds and would be able to return to her regiment, but and most importantly; she was going to see Yuri.

The colonel called for the two soldiers who had treated her so roughly to take her to the truck waiting outside. This time the soldiers gently took her arms and assisted her down the steps to the awaiting truck and Yuri. "Sorry, comrade. Very sorry," they both kept saying to Vera.

Yuri jumped out of the ambulance truck and hurried toward Vera. "Help her get into the truck," he ordered the two soldiers. Carefully, they assisted her into the back of the ambulance where a single stretcher had been placed. Yuri climbed into the back with her and ordered the two soldiers to close the doors. He signaled the driver to get moving.

The truck lurched and began to move down the cobbled streets to the military hospital.

Yuri gently took Vera's hands and turned them over. He reached into a large, canvas bag and pulled out ointments and clean cloths. When he looked into her face, he saw the tears rolling down her face. "I never thought I would see you again," she said.

His eyes filled with tears, too. "When our troops came in and freed the prisoners, I was forced to flee at gun point with the German SS Colonel. He wanted his own physician for him and his family. It took our troops two days to catch up to this loathsome man and free me. The colonel was shot trying to escape and killed. I do not know what happened to his wife and child. My first concern was to find you. When I finally found out where you had been taken, I could not believe it. I tried to get you out of there. I tried and tried for days."

Vera pulled herself up on her elbows. "Please hold me," she said weeping.

Yuri got on his knees and gently took her in his arms. "My dearest, brave little Vera."

"What would have happened to me if you had not tried to free me?" Vera asked as he held her tightly.

He pulled back and smiled. "I would never have stopped trying to get you free. Never." His hand reached up and brushed a loose curl on her forehead. "I think while you are recovering in the hospital it would be a good idea to marry. Do you not agree?"

"With all my heart," she grabbed him and pulled her to him. She did not feel the pain of her hands or leg, only the ecstasy of being held by Yuri.

"I have been assigned to this military hospital until my orders come through for my next assignment," he shrugged. "So, let us take advantage of this small window of time to be with each other."

"I will take whatever time we can steal to be together," she said stroking his cheek against the back of her burnt hand.

* * *

Vera and Yuri married three days after they arrived at the military hospital.

The hospital staff found an unused, small utility room at the hospital that they made into a room for Vera and Yuri. Luckily, it had a very thin window that opened, and just enough room for a large, single bed to be squeezed into it. Vera thought it was a palace.

It took three months for all of Vera's wounds to heal completely. The worst and most painful part were getting her severely burnt hands to work normally again.

One day, Yuri came into the small room they shared together in the hospital. "My darling," he said sadly. "Your orders came in today for you to leave for your regiment immediately. And I have been posted to the front lines again."

"I had almost forgotten that we are still at war," Vera sighed deeply. "At times I have felt guilty that I have not been there to help my comrades fight. But mostly, I feel guilty because I have never known such happiness when all around us there is so much death and pain. I have never felt so loved and been so deeply in love."

"This war cannot last forever, and then we will be free to be with each other," he said as he gently stroked her hair and face.

"Yes," Vera said emphatically. "I believe that with all my heart."

Yuri left the following day, and the day after that Vera was sent back to her old regiment where she was greeted with hugs and kisses from the entire regiment.

Chapter 15

Vera soon found herself easily getting back into the swing of flying and dropping bombs over enemy soldiers every few minutes.

She was grateful that the sub-zero weather was gone, and that spring had finally arrived. However, along with spring came the rains and winds.

One morning the night bombers returned to their dugouts to grab their much-needed sleep. No sooner had they all fallen onto their plank beds when one of the mechanics raced into their quarters screaming for them to get up. They were needed on the field because the rain and wind had kicked up so badly their planes were being blown around.

Everyone scrambled to their plane. Pilots, navigators and mechanics all crawled up on both wings of their plane and fell prone. The top wings gave very little protection to the women from the wet wind as it began to saturate every bit of clothing they wore. They all stayed on the wings of their planes until the winds died down a couple of hours later. Soaking wet, all the women headed back to their quarters. Except the mechanics who had to stay on the field and finish repairing and preparing for that night's flight out.

Rimma and Larissa were glad they had Vera and her plane back to take care of and were even happier that their new airfield was near a little village. That meant they could go into town and trade things, like the men's underwear that was issued to them, for food. On one of their trips, Rimma and Larissa were loaded down with bread, potatoes and fresh apricots when the Assistant Deputy Commander stopped them on the road back to the airfield.

"How did you come by these items?" She demanded.

"Comrade Assistant Deputy Commander Vrtika," Larissa smiled. "We just took the male underwear they issued us and traded them for all of this wonderful food we can all share."

"Yes," Rimma chimed in. "We women never wore these things and thought we could put them to better use by getting us some good food in exchange for them"

"All we did was move the men's underwear from base to base anyway, and they were just dirty rags to us," Larissa said.

"When I return to base, report to my office immediately," the assistant deputy commander ordered. Her dark-brown hair was pulled back into a severe bun, and her small, black eyes set close together, over her long, pinched nose. Her thin lips held a nasty smirk as she gestured for them to return to the base.

Rimma and Larissa stood looking after the commander puzzled by her reactions. "Maybe she wants this food all to herself," Rimma shrugged.

"Come on." Larissa muttered, as they walked back to their base.

When the assistant deputy commander returned, Rimma and Larissa were already there waiting for her.

"Do you realize the severity of your crime?" She asked the startled women.

"You mean trading the men's underwear?" Rimma asked.

"The rags?" Larissa interjected.

"That was government property, nevertheless. I caught you in the act and have found you guilty of stealing government property during wartime and the penalty is ten years in Siberia," she snapped. She motioned for two of the women on patrol to take them to holding cells until they could be shipped out to Siberia.

The cell for each of them was a large wooden box that they could not sit or lay down in. They were let out periodically to go to the toilet and to eat their food, as it was too tight in their boxes to raise their arms.

Vera had not been on base when this event had occurred with her mechanics. She had taken the base commander, Major Korkavic on a three-day mission.

When she returned Katrina quickly told Vera about Rimma and Larissa. Vera raced to the major and informed him of what had happened and pleaded for her friends. She ended by saying that there were not too many mechanics on the field as good as Rimma and Larissa.

* * *

The major shook his head and growled, "I will take care of this issue comrade. You have been up for two nights and must fly again tonight. Get some sleep. That is an order."

Sr. Major Kashmir Korkavic stood for a while looking out of his window. He watched all the mechanics frantically working on badly damaged planes. His heart went out to the ground crews he had come to respect. They worked hours upon hours without sleep and in the freezing cold, sleet, heat and anything else nature threw at them. Their faces and fingers were frost-bitten in the winter and in the summer, the mosquitoes feasted on them day and night. They slept in foxholes, under the wings of their planes and anywhere else they could grab a little sleep. He never heard one of them complain.

At first, he was offended to be assigned to an all-female regiment, but now he felt it was an honor to work with these brave, fearless women. They were overworked, undernourished and had very little sleep.

He had been a fighter pilot and was so badly wounded it took him months to re-cooperate. His leg never healed right, and he was not eligible to fly in combat anymore.

"Comrade Katrina," he yelled. "Get in here. We have some work to do."

A couple of hours later, Major Korkavic and Katrina had made all the calls necessary to solve the problem they had at the base.

"I believe we have rectified the problem here at the base, do you not agree, Comrade Katrina?"

Katrina broke into a huge grin, "Yes, Comrade Major; I believe we have."

"Good, then have someone get Comrade Deputy Commander Vrtika immediately."

"I believe she is in her quarter's sleeping. She has not slept much in the last three days. She said she was exhausted and really needed some sleep." Katrina paused for a moment and then excitedly asked, "Can I wake her up? Please. Comrade Major Korkavic,"

"Good, yes! Wake her up and tell her to respond here immediately." He smiled at the thought of her sleep being interrupted. She had been transferred to his base six months ago, and he thought her abrasive and cold in manner. As time went on he found her to be harsh, cruel and unreasonable with the women and not suited for duty at his base or any base for that matter.

A couple of minutes later, Assistant Deputy Commander Vrtika appeared before his desk.

He skipped the formality of greetings with her. "I see you have charged and convicted two of our mechanics to Siberia for ten years for trading men's underwear for food."

She thrust out her chest and her voice filled with pride, "Yes. It was I and I alone that had those violators arrested."

"I see," his jaw tightened from anger, but he managed to keep it out of his voice. "You are a very good Assistant Deputy Commander Vrtika, and I feel your talents and shall I say, an 'eye for detail' that is wasted on this base."

He watched as she let a smug smile cross her face. The commander wanted to get rid of her, but some place that would keep her so busy she would not have time to see if her prisoners ever made it to Siberia.

"I have some contacts in Stalingrad, and they have need for a prudent, dedicated and sharp officer in charge of procuring supplies to our soldiers. Is this a position that you could fulfill?" He asked, knowing very well that she wanted a position where she was in command.

"I would be honored to take such a position to help our Motherland." She held her head high and spoke with great dramatics.

"They are going to be in for a surprise to have such an officer like you, Comrade Captain Vrtika," he saluted her and smiled.

"When do I leave, Comrade Commander?" She saluted back and asked excitedly.

"Right now," he said. "Grab your belongings. I believe this is a perfect fit for you and your talents. Our assistant, Comrade Katrina has already ordered a plane for you." They saluted each other.

She turned and raced out of his office barking at Katrina that her plane had better be ready for takeoff immediately.

"Immediately, if not sooner," the major sighed. He waited until she was on the plane and in the sky before he called Katrina to walk with him over to where the two mechanics were imprisoned.

"Release them," he ordered the two female guards who were standing in front of their cells.

"Yes, sir," they said bewildered, and at the same time anxious to release their two friends. They opened the doors, and the two mechanics came out of their individual boxes.

"Comrade Sr. Major Korkavic are we being taken to Siberia now? We understand what we did was wrong, and we deserve this punishment." Rimma said seriously. She held up a hand to block the not so bright light outside because it hurt her eyes from being held in the dark cell.

"I believe you have been in these prison boxes for three days. Is that correct?" He grabbed Rimma's arm to steady her body that was swaying slightly.

"Yes, Comrade Major," they both replied.

"I believe that is a just punishment for the crime," he shook his head at the terrible prison boxes. "I order you to your quarters to get some much-needed sleep."

"But Assistant Deputy Commander Vrtika said we have to go to Siberia for ten years," Larissa sounded confused.

"Comrade Assistant Deputy Commander Vrtika has been reassigned. She will not be coming back to our base." He stood there looking at the two women who were just staring at him and not moving. "If you like I can send you two to Siberia, or you can get to your quarters, get some sleep, and then be ready to get back to work."

"Yes, Comrade Major," they both said at the same time and took off walking as best they could from being cramped up in the boxes.

Major Korkavic stood for a moment looking over the boxes that were used to punish the women. "I have no idea who thought this was a good idea to punish the women, or to punish anyone. And, I had no idea they were being used. Katrina, and you two, help me with this," he ordered the two sentries that had been guarding Rimma and Larissa.

The four of them pushed the two prison cell boxes over. "I want these dismantled for good. We will find a more suitable and less inhumane place of confinement for our prisoners," he snapped.

A few hours later, the pilot who had taken the Assistant Deputy Commander Vrtika to Stalingrad came to his office. "Comrade Vrtika has been delivered to Stalingrad safely. She was very excited to report to her new post in Stalingrad."

"Stalingrad?" He feigned ignorance.

"Why, yes, Comrade Major, that is where she said she was going to be stationed."

"That will be all Comrade Lt. Markovich." He saluted and gave a half smile.

Katrina waited until the pilot was gone and closed the door to the major's office.

"Oh, I must have forgotten to tell her the part about her being taken to Stalingrad and then flown to Siberia. She will be in command of procuring uniforms and equipment for the soldiers who are stationed there for the remainder of the war. Comrade Katrina, did I forget to mention that minor detail to Commander Vrtika?"

A big grin spread across her pretty face, "Yes, Comrade Commander; I think you did forget to tell her about that."

"Hmm, what an oversight on my part."

* * *

A couple of days later the major was out inspecting the planes on the airfield.

Larissa nudged Rimma, "Here he comes."

"Stop it," Rimma said slightly annoyed. "He does not inspect the planes just to see me."

"You are the only one in the whole regiment that does not see he has feelings for you," Larissa shook her head. "You may be a great mechanic, but you are a dunce when it comes to men. When we came out of our prison cells the other day, I was unsteady on my feet, too, but he took your arm not mine."

"He just did not see that you were unsteady, too." She replied convinced she was right.

"I could have fallen over on my face, and he would have stepped over me to help you," Larissa stated flatly. "So, do you not have any feelings for the major? You are the only one on the airfield that does not drool when he comes around."

"I find him very attractive. And," she sighed, "I do care about him quite a bit," Rimma said. "But loving someone during a war is a stupid thing. I was in love with a young soldier when the war first started; he was killed a month later. I refuse to let my heart be torn apart again."

The major made his last stop, as was his usual routine, by Vera's plane where Rimma was busy doing the repairs.

"Comrade Rimma," he called to her. "I would like a word with you."

Rimma jumped off the wing where she was putting a replacement panel and stood next to him. "Yes, Comrade Major?"

He motioned for her to walk with him away from the plane. "I would like to ask you a personal question," his voice rang with nervousness. "If I may have your permission to speak?"

"Yes, Comrade Major," Rimma said. "What is it?"

"I would like to know your feeling toward me," he blurted it out so fast Rimma almost did not understand him.

Rimma glanced away from him for a moment and when she looked back into his eyes, she knew Larissa was right; he did care for her.

"Comrade Major," she spoke softly. "I care about you very much. Alright, too much. But I will not let myself become involved with someone until after the war. It hurts too much when they die. When there is peace once again in the Motherland then, and only then, will I totally belong to someone."

"Fair enough," a large grin spread across his face. "Until the end of the war." He walked her back to her plane. "Thank you, Comrade Rimma," and walked briskly away.

Chapter 16

Vera was now fully recovered and had been very anxious to get back to her regiment and help in the war effort, but at the same time she felt guilty. She wanted to forget about the war and spend the rest of her life with Yuri. When she would receive one of his letters, she would hold it to her heart and close her eyes hoping that when she opened her eyes, he would be there standing in front of her. But he wasn't, so she just took solace in the love pouring from his letters. Clutching his letter over her heart, she fell asleep, until she felt someone shaking her.

"Comrade Vera," Ksenia said, gently shaking Vera awake. "You have new orders."

"We have been flying for twelve hours straight," she sighed and looked at her watch. "I have only slept three hours. What are our orders now?"

"Not 'our' orders, but yours," she said. "You have to fly a colonel to the front lines again. He flew in last night while we were on one of our sorties and needs to be flown to the airfield near Kiev. And, you have not been sleeping three hours, just two."

"All right," Vera dropped her feet over the edge of her plank bed. "I am just so very tired lately."

"Could it be because we are lucky if we average three to four hours of sleep a day?" Ksenia walked over to her bed and sat down.

"That much?" Vera arched her back, yawned and slowly got up.

"I see you got another letter from Yuri," Ksenia sat looking at the letter in Vera's hand. "It has been almost three months since you last saw him."

"I know and I miss him every waking moment," Vera grabbed her flight jacket, leather cap and gloves.

"That would be a lot of 'waking moments' for you at this point," Ksenia watched as her friend pulled back the canvas door and walked out of the shelter.

Vera hurried to the base headquarters and was greeted by a general, and the base commander, Sr. Major Kashmir Korkavic, who was walking toward her.

"Comrade Sr. Captain Vera Dreklin will be your pilot," Major Korkavic said gesturing toward Vera. "She is probably the best pilot on the base."

"I am sure they are all competent," Colonel General Petravich smiled politely. He was short and thin with a thick mustache over his full lips.

"Comrade Colonel General Petravich," Vera spoke up. "Thank you. All the pilots are very competent and excellent fliers. It would be an honor to take you where you need to go."

The general turned to the major. "Comrade Major Korkavic," he saluted. "If ever you need my assistance, please do not hesitate. For the Motherland."

"Yes, for the Motherland," the major returned the salute and nodded to Vera. "Sr. Captain Dreklin, I had your mechanics refuel and fix your plane. It is ready for takeoff. Please escort the general to your plane and have a safe flight."

Rimma and Larissa were standing at attention as the general and Vera walked up to the plane.

He stopped and gasped for a moment, "These are your mechanics? Women?"

"Yes, Comrade General," Vera said respectfully.

"Everything has been fixed," Rimma walked with Vera as she inspected the plane. "We replaced two valves and we worked on the throttle. The fuselage was damaged, but just a little by the flak. It is all fixed and the damage to the underside of the plane, too." She looked directly at the stunned officer.

"We managed to patch up most of the holes in the wings and a couple of bullet holes that tore through the front seat," Larissa shook her head. "You were very lucky this flight that you were not hit by any of the rifle fire, machine guns or flak during your eighth run dropping bombs on the fascist pigs last night."

Vera hid the smile that was trying to cross her face. She knew the two mechanics were explaining how many flights she had made that night and the danger she went through for the ranking officer's benefit. She winked at the two mechanics and saluted them. "Thank you for your hard work." She motioned for the general to get into the plane.

He stood for a moment looking at the plane he was about to ride in. "Why have they not mounted machine guns to fight off an attack? How can you women protect yourselves?"

"She does it every night, Comrade General," Rimma said.

"Are there no fighter planes on this field to fly along with you for protection?" His voice filled with concern.

"No sir," Vera said somewhat surprised by the general's interest in their safety. "The PO-2 is all we have."

"When I get back to my base I will see if there is anything I can do. I cannot promise you anything, but I will try," he said. "Well, you may not have a machine gun this trip, but I have a pistol," he laughed. "Unfortunately, it will be of little use."

Rimma held out the parachute for the general and tried to help him adjust it. "Excuse me, Comrade General," she said working one of the straps. "I am still not quite familiar with adjusting the parachutes."

Vera saw the bewildered look on the general's face as she climbed into her cockpit. "They have just given us parachutes in our planes."

"Do you mean you have been flying all this time without them?" He yelled in disbelief.

"Yes sir, we were not given any parachutes until just recently," Vera looked down and smiled at the parachute pack she was sitting on. It raised her higher than her pillow, so she had better visibility.

One final adjustment and the general's parachute was secured. "I find it totally unacceptable that you women are not given the proper equipment. All of our bomber and fighter units have parachutes and you women do not." Vera saw his jaw tighten as he hoisted himself up on the wing of the plane and climbed into the rear cockpit.

Vera waited until the propeller was wound, and the engine revved up and started down the field.

It was a sunny day with thick clouds sporadically clustered above, as Vera flew toward Kiev. Their flight was going well until Vera spotted two Messerschmitts flying toward them. The spotty, cloud cover overhead was their only chance of survival against the German fighter planes. Vera pushed the throttle back and began climbing toward the clouds.

The general leaned forward and touched her shoulder. "What is happening?" he yelled into her ear.

Vera raised her arm and pointed to the two planes that were bearing down on them. She hoped that the sun shining on the German planes' windshield gave them enough time to seek cloud cover before they were spotted. She also knew that most German fighters did not like to fly in clouds, so she flew her plane deep into the clouds.

"How long can we stay up here?" The colonel asked.

She looked back to him. "We need to listen to their engines to determine when they are gone."

The German aircraft flew very close and slowly the sound of their engines faded until they could not be heard anymore. Vera had flown high and deep into the clouds now she quickly surfaced below them. The German fighters were nowhere to be seen. Her engines began to purr as she headed back on course to deliver the anxious colonel.

The rest of her trip was uneventful. She landed the colonel safely.

"Well, Comrade Sr. Lieutenant," he said patting her shoulder. "That was very good flying up there. I am grateful I had you as a pilot. I will see what I can do for your regiment," he climbed onto the wing and jumped down. He looked up at Vera, who had climbed out of her cockpit and was standing on the wing of her plane and saluted her.

Vera returned the salute and watched him walk away. "Why are there not more officers like him? He really knows that a woman is capable of doing what a man can do."

Vera sat on the wing of her plane and watched as the mechanics worked feverishly on getting the fighter planes nearby ready for take-off. They fueled and prepped the plane as they checked and rechecked their work.

Most of the mechanics were men, but she spotted two female mechanics that were just finishing up their work. They patted each other on the back and were laughing when they spotted her sitting on the wing.

Both women hurried over to her and introduced themselves as Sr. Sgt. Maria Aresko and Sgt. Zoya Rosno.

Vera was startled by the distinct difference in appearance of the two mechanics. Zoya was a very tiny woman, but Maria was extremely tall. Maria was looking her directly in the eyes, and she was sitting on the wing of her plane.

"You fly the 'duckling'," Maria ran her hand over the wing. Her eyes ran over the little Biplane with great interest.

"We have heard and seen them flying around a lot, but we have never had time to look at one," Zoya strained to see into the cockpit.

"Hop up and take a look." Vera moved off the wing so they both could get up and check it out. "When you are done is it possible for me to get some petrol?"

"We can do that now," Maria said happily. She glanced over her shoulder and spotted Sophie walking toward her plane. "Comrade Sr. Captain Cherkov look who has dropped in for a visit."

Sophie gestured for the men she was walking with to keep moving and headed toward Maria, Zoya and Vera. Her face lit up when she saw Vera standing there. "Comrade Sr. Captain Zhkov, it is so good to see you again."

"Comrade Senior Captain Cherkov," Vera opened her arms and the two women embraced quickly. She stood back, smiled and said proudly, "I am now Sr. Captain Dreklin."

"Wonderful news," Sophie said. "I do not think I want to fall in love until after the war. There will be plenty of time after the war. I hope."

"I must admit love took me by surprise," Vera laughed and changed the subject. "Are you preparing to fly out now?"

"Yes, I was on my way to my plane when I spotted you," she pointed to an aircraft not far from them.

"Do you still have an all-woman crew?"

"No," she said. "Can you believe it - I have an all-male flight crew now. But I am still the pilot. It took them a while to realize that a woman can pilot one of these things and do it well."

"I do not think the men will ever accept us women as pilots," Vera said disgustedly.

"You are right on that point," she chuckled. "I could tell you horror stories about my encounters with the male ranking officers."

"I have had a couple of those just recently," Vera smiled.

"Well, it has been wonderful talking with you," Sophie pointed to her waiting crew. "I must get to my plane and get into the air. We have had reports of the German fighters' loitering near the Black Sea making it difficult to get anyone in and out. So, now we must fly to clear the air space so that they can get some of our higher-ranking officers safely away."

"Fly safe, Comrade." Vera gave Sophie a quick hug good-bye.

"You as well, Comrade." Sophie waved back.

Chapter 17

Sophie hurried to catch up to her crew walking toward their plane.

"Exchanging cooking tips or beauty tips," Lt. Iosif Sokavich said to Sophie with sarcasm dripping from each of his words.

"No," Sophie replied icily. "We were discussing how to kill some males without getting caught. It was quite enlightening."

"No problem," he spoke as if quite bored. "Just have them fly with a woman pilot."

"You, too," she quipped angrily. "Why did I think you were different than most of the other males?"

"Because I am, Comrade," he smiled charmingly at her.

His rugged good looks and dimpled smile always made her mad, and she had no idea why.

"You know I am making a joke. I find you somewhat competent as a pilot."

"For a moment, I thought you were going to say something nice," she brushed past him and climbed into their plane. "It must have been a very stupid moment for me. A common mistake on my part."

"Comrade, there is nothing stupid about you," he smiled at her. His blue eyes were alive with humor. "And, there is nothing common about you in any way. Look, I am holding out my heart to you. Can you see it?" He held out his up turned hands.

Sophie turned and looked at the empty hands of Iosif. "Ah, you have proven my point. You have no heart as your hands are empty. Now let us get into the air. We have lost time with your nonsense," she ordered.

"Yes, Comrade Sr. Lt. your copilot is on top of you." He began working the levers and switches from his seat behind her.

"What?"

"What? What?" he asked feigning innocence for his remark. "I am sitting behind you on top of the situation. What did you think I meant?"

"We have been flying together for five months, and I know exactly what you meant," she said sharply. She wanted to be angry at him but could not and smiled despite the situation. There were so many incidents and comments where she could have brought him up on insubordination, but he was the glue that held her crew together. He brought his intelligence and wit to every altercation they encountered, and she felt it would be a waste to send this annoying man to prison.

They taxied down the runway and flew into the cloudless sky. It wasn't long before Sophie saw the sky fill with their fighter bombers. She maneuvered her plane at the designated altitude as they headed for the Black Sea.

Their destination was a couple of miles away when the radio communication officer radioed that the planes carrying their packages, meaning the high-ranking officers, were straight ahead.

Sophie and the rest of the regiment circled around and formed a protective shield around the two planes that held the officers. Everything was going as planned until several German Focke-Wulfs fighters broke from the clouds.

Sophie, her crew and several other planes were assigned as fighters in case of an attack. Five fighter planes led the two planes with the officers away from the fight.

One of the Focke-Wulf's saw the seven planes moving away from the rest of the fighters and dove down toward it. Sophie spotted the well-armed, fast enemy plane and chased after it. She pushed the throttle to full power and came up under the belly of the plane. The gunner and Iosif began firing at the powerful and fast German fighter. The enemy plane swung around, as did Iosif in his swiveling, machine gun chair. "Come on, just a little bit more," he screamed.

Then his machine gun came alive as he began firing in short concentrated bursts at the approaching enemy. Spent shells pinged and sprayed all over the cockpit as he continued firing until the German fighter was hit and began to spiral down with a white plume of smoke following behind it.

Another enemy fighter came in from the side sending bullets into the cockpit ricocheting against the steel plates. Sophie's radio operator opened fire and hit the plane killing the pilot instantly.

The sky was swarming with Focke-Wulfs as Sophie moved to get a better advantage of another enemy fighter coming in for an attack.

"We have one coming in from the rear," Iosif yelled.

"There is one coming at us from the front," she screamed back to him. "Hold on to something."

"I am. My butt," he yelled to her. "I am going to kiss it good-bye if you do not do something now."

Enemy rounds were hitting their wings and zinging off metal as Sophie stayed their course. Suddenly, Sophie pushed down on the throttle causing the plane to dive sharply. She immediately split off from the two enemy planes. Her evasive action was so fast and unexpected the two enemy planes collided in mid-air. The explosion from the two planes caused their plane to waver from the turbulence, and it felt like something struck their plane. "Iosif," Sophie screamed back to him. "The throttle is stuck. I cannot move it."

Iosif jumped down from the bubbled dome and grabbed the throttle with Sophie. They pushed and pulled on the throttle until they heard a slight pinging sound and immediately the throttle seemed to be released. Just then an enemy fighter swooped down and sent a barrage of bullets through the cockpit.

Sophie screamed as she saw Iosif fall. She swayed and turned to get the enemy off her tail. The throttle stick was starting to act up again, and her heart was pounding as she saw the enemy plane line up for its kill.

Suddenly, the enemy plane burst into flames and disappeared from her view. She looked over and saw one of the other Soviet pilot's waggle his wings. Sophie smiled and saluted him in a gesture of thank you.

The dogfight was over, as the enemy planes changed directions and flew off. Sophie leveled off her plane and headed back to her airfield with the other Soviet planes.

While they flew back to the airfield, Sophie kept calling Iosif's name. He was not responding. She couldn't leave her post as pilot, and the radio had been knocked out during one of the strafing's, the only thing she could do was get back to the airfield as fast as she could.

The plane shook and shuddered the entire flight back to base. It took every ounce of strength she had to try to land the plane without crashing it. She tried to release the landing wheels, but they were jammed. Sophie worried that her radio operator and tail gunner would be killed, if they weren't already dead, if she landed on the cement runway. She could smell petrol permeating the cockpit and knew one little spark, and they would explode on impact or be burnt alive.

Quickly, she sized up the situation and opted to land on the grassy field that ran along-side of the runway. She had to keep the nose of the plane up or none of them would make it. Sophie eased the throttle into landing position and fought to keep it straight.

The plane hit the grass-covered field hard, jarring her to the core. She still held on to the throttle. Her knuckles were white from gripping it so tightly, but nothing seemed to be slowing the plane down.

They had traveled for what seemed like forever when her plane finally stopped. She stared in complete shock. Two more feet and their plane would have been sent sliding down a steep, rocky ravine.

Her first instinct was to get the wounded out of the plane before it exploded.

The gunner was being helped out of the tail of the plane by the radio operator. "Quickly, get out and away from the plane," she ordered. Her attention turned to Iosif, who was unconscious on the floor of the cockpit. She raced to his side and knelt beside him. Blood was everywhere on his face. She wanted to scream, but instead she grabbed him under his shoulders and began pulling him from the plane.

He was much bigger and heavier than she was, and she didn't know what to do when Iosef moaned.

"Iosef," she cried out. "Please help me get you out of this plane."

Blood was rushing down his face as he stumbled to his feet. Together they climbed out of the plane and onto the wing. As they jumped off the wing, Iosef collapsed to the ground on his hands and knees.

Sophie knelt beside him, "You have to help me, my Iosef."

Iosef pushed himself to a standing position as Sophie quickly got under one arm and helped support him away from the damaged plane.

There was a small cluster of trees far enough from the plane where they would be safe until they were rescued. Sophie knew that their rescue trucks would be hurrying toward their position.

Finally, Sophie got Iosef to the trees where his body slumped to the ground, and she collapsed down next to him.

The radio operator and gunner made it safely to the tree line, too. She called out to see how badly they were hurt. They said it was mostly superficial wounds, and they would be all right.

Relief washed over her as she looked up and saw their rescue trucks racing toward them.

Her attention was diverted back to Iosif. "Help is coming. Help is coming. You will be fine, Iosif," she said tenderly. "Hold on. I order you not to die."

Iosif moaned, and Sophie sat up and leaned over him. He moaned again.

"What are you trying to say?" She asked with tears forming in her eyes.

"Kiss me before I die, my Sophie" he pleaded weakly.

"What?" She asked incredulously.

"Kiss me before I die," he said a little stronger.

"You fool. You foolish man." Sophie said as she leaned down and kissed him gently on the lips.

The trucks pulled up to Sophie and the others. Some of the men ran toward the plane, and others were pulling stretchers from the truck.

"Hurry," she stood up and began waving and yelling to the medics. "Please hurry."

Sophie was stunned when the medics raced by her and Iosif. She looked down and saw that Iosif was smiling and waving his hand toward the wounded gunner and radio operator.

"What the hell?" Sophie said, and she had never sworn in her life before.

"I thought it was more like heaven myself," he sighed deeply and over exaggeratedly.

"You are injured. You are dying," she exclaimed.

"Not today my fair lady, not today," he went to stand up and fell back down. "I might be a little dizzy here though. A little help here." He motioned with his hand for Sophie to help him stand up.

"Medic!" Sophie growled. "This Comrade idiot needs some help."

"Aw, come on," Iosif said cheerfully. "I did get a nasty bump on my head."

"Nasty bump?" Sophie wanted to scream at him, but a medic was by his side wiping away the blood from his forehead.

"I was dodging a stream of bullets and hit my head on the metal plate behind your chair. Knocked me out cold I guess."

"He only has a little gash," the medic stood up. "He will be fine."

"Not after I shoot him," Sophie said. She flounced to one of the trucks and sat down.

All the way back to the base headquarters Iosif tried to speak to Sophie, but she ignored him.

There was a lot of commotion going on when Sophie returned to base. All the generals had been flown out, except one general who remained at the base. He had wanted to meet and thank all the senior officers who had so valiantly protected him and the other high-ranking officers during their flight from the front lines. Sophie excused herself so that she could freshen up first and arrived at the meeting a few minutes late.

The men stood when she entered the room. "Ah, very pretty. Very pretty, indeed," said the tall, balding officer. His had a pinched face, and his beady eyes kept sizing Sophie up and down, which made her very uncomfortable. "I am General Hrtova. And as a thank you for getting me back here safely I have invited all the senior officers to a dinner I am planning tonight. I am sorry your base commander has been called away and shall miss it. You will join us of course," he ordered more than asked Sophie.

"Yes, of course," Sophie felt honored to be asked to join all the male officers at a dinner.

"You do have a dress or something better to look at than that smelly uniform, do you not?" He asked wrinkling his nose at the smell of grease, petrol, and smoke.

"Yes, of course," Sophie said feeling she spoke too soon about it being an honored to join him. She disliked him instantly. After what seemed forever listening to the general and other officers talking war business Sophie felt she had stayed the proper length of time and excused herself.

"We shall eat at 1800 hours," the general called to her as she was walking out the door.

Iosif was waiting outside the commander center with a small bandage stuck over his wound. "What was that all about?" Iosif asked.

"I have been asked to join the officers for dinner tonight. If it is any of your business, which it is not," she said flippantly.

She hurried away from him and entered her quarters. Sophie needed to wash up and find something womanly to wear. She had no dresses, but she found a military skirt she could wear in its place.

1800 hours came quickly for Sophie, and she was led into the general's quarters where the officers were standing around shifting their feet. Not one of them looked her in the eyes.

Sophie was delighted that there were meat and potatoes on the table. The general had her sit next to him and filled her wine glass to the brim. The conversation at the table was stilted and Sophie thought the officers ate rather quickly, and as soon as they were done, one by one they excused themselves.

Thinking that the officers were giving her a clue to leave as well, she stood up to go, but the general grabbed her hand and pulled her back down on her chair.

"No, I want you to stay." His hand dropped on her knee and began to move up her skirt.

Sophie jumped up, "Thank you Comrade General for the most delicious of meals. But I have an early flight tomorrow, and I must get my sleep."

"I could arrange to have you sleep here," he smiled and got up from his chair. He walked around the table sizing her up and down. "You are quite a lovely little thing. I cannot believe you play with those big planes. I have something more interesting for you to play with."

Sophie knew exactly what he meant. She was at a loss as what to do. He was bigger and stronger than her, and she knew she couldn't fight him off for long.

Suddenly, there was a loud pounding on the general's door.

"Who is it?" The general yelled agitatedly. "I gave orders that I do not wish to be disturbed."

The door opened, and Iosif was standing there. He gave an over-exaggerated salute and smiled. "It is just me, Comrade General. I was just worried about my wife."

"Your wife?" The general stood there with his mouth open.

"Yes, Comrade General, she is expecting our child. I saw everyone leave but her, and I thought maybe she might have gotten sick again."

"Sick again?" The general was repeating Iosif's words in a total stupor.

"Well," he winked at the general. "Just between us men, Comrade General, she not only throws up a lot, but she has gas. I mean really bad gas at times." He waved his hand in front of his face as if he smelled something bad.

"I..." The general stumbled for words.

"I want to thank you Comrade General for taking such good care of her, but I think I had better get her out of here," Iosif looked over at the table with some of the food still on it. "Oh, yes. I had better get her out of here before one or the other end of her starts erupting."

"Thank you, Comrade General, for the wonderful meal," Sophie said as she brushed past him and hurried out the door.

"Good evening, Comrade General," Iosif saluted, turned and walked out of the stunned general's quarters shutting the door behind him. He hurried after Sophie, who had run down the airfield. Iosif caught up to her and grabbed her arm. When he turned her around, there were tears falling down her face

Sophie threw her arms around Iosif. Her body was trembling. "If you had not come in."

"But I did," he said holding her tightly to him. "Come on. We can sit on our poor beat up plane's wing. We do not need the general finding either one of us tonight." He put his arm around her waist as they walked to their plane while Sophie rested her head on his shoulder.

They got to their plane, but the mechanics were busy working on it. Maria looked at Sophie's face and Iosif's arm around her. "Oh, the dinner with that creepy general. The food was not to your liking, huh." But the tone in her voice indicated she knew it was not the food, but the general who had caused the problem. "The plane at the end of the field," she pointed way down the airfield. "It did not fly out today, and nobody is around it."

Iosif mouthed the words 'thank you' and guided Sophie down to the last plane on the runway.

They crawled onto the wing of the plane and sat down. "This plane is far enough away from prying eyes or ears," Iosif said keeping his arm around Sophie.

"Do Generals get away with things like that?" Sophie finally spoke.

"Who can stop them?" Iosif tightened his arm around Sophie.

Sophie looked into his face and smiled, "You can. Thank you, Iosif. Thank you." She leaned over and kissed him on the lips.

He returned her kiss and when their kiss ended he put his forehead to hers. "We are going to have to come up with a story about why we did not obtain permission from our base commander to marry."

She reached up and touched his cheek and pulled back looking into his eyes for the first time. She could feel the love pouring out from his blue eyes into her very soul.

"I love you Sophie." He gently touched her cheek.

"I love you, too." She laid her head against his shoulder.

"You not just saying that because I saved you from the General are you?"

Sophie responded in a serious voice, "Yes."

"What?" He asked incredulously pulling away from her.

She laughed, "No. It is not because of that horrible general. I have been in love with you for a while, but I fought it because I did not want to fall in love during this awful war."

"I knew you could not resist my charms, although you had me going there for a while."

"Iosif, I have a thought about this marriage thing," Sophie said with enthusiasm. "There are so many destroyed villages and all the birth and marriage records were destroyed along with them. So, let us pick a town that has been destroyed, and we can make up a time and when."

"I was hoping you had a different solution, like us getting really married," he sighed.

Sophie dropped her head down and was very quiet.

"Just wishful thinking," he said with sadness filling his voice.

"I will marry you, Iosif. I will marry you anywhere and anytime. Forget about the war. We should grab a little corner of happiness wherever we can find it." She took his face in her hands. "I love you, my Iosif."

He grabbed her and kissed her with a passion she had never known. When the kiss ended Iosif fell back against the wing of the plane. "Woman, you are something," he reached up and gently pulled her down to him. "Come lie beside me for a moment."

They laid there for a while holding each other and not saying a word.

"I have it," Iosif said. "We shall tell them the city we married in, time and place, but it will be a city that has been destroyed of course, and in the meantime we will get married by the first city official we can find. An official where that morally, degenerate general will never find out about."

"What if they ask us where we met?"

"We have a few hours to come up with collaborating stories," he laughed. "We can make it really good."

"I will worry about you sitting behind me unprotected," Sophie became glum for a moment.

"Do you know how I really got this bump on my head?"

"You hit it on the back of my seat," she cocked her head and looked at him.

"I was diving to cover you from the bullets and slipped on some of the bullet casings." He fussed with the collar of her pilot's jacket. "I fear for you every time we climb into that plane." Worry etched its way across his face.

"I worry about all of us," she glanced down shyly, "but, especially you."

"We are a good team, my love," he said smiling at her.

Sophie propped herself up on her elbow. She looked down at him, and then playfully nudged his shoulder. "Pregnant, throwing up and bad gas. Really?"

"It worked did it not. The look on the general's face was worth every moment," he laughed heartily and pulled her to him again. "Come here you throwing up, gassed up women."

They stayed together until the cold began to chill them to the bone. "I hate to say this, but I think we had better get back to our quarters." He gently brushed away a lock of hair the wind had blown across her face. "Until tomorrow, my love." He leaned over and kissed her passionately.

"Until tomorrow," she replied.

"I fear you did not finish that sentence," he jested.

"My love." Sophie shook her head. "I never thought I would ever say those words to anyone."

"I knew you were going to say them to me," he laughed smugly.

"Well, I am glad one of us did." She reached up and pulled his face close to hers. "Kiss me, you crazy fool."

His eyes became almost a dark blue as he studied her face for a moment. He pulled her to him and held her gently before he kissed her again. When the kiss ended, he jumped down off the wing and held his arms for her.

Slowly, they walked back to their separate quarters. They hugged each other tightly and said their good nights.

In the morning, they were both relieved when they saw the general getting on a plane and leaving their base.

The base commander had returned from his mission and called Sophie and Iosif in separately.

Iosif went in first and then Sophie. After a few minutes, Sophie came out of his office to find Iosif waiting for her.

"What did he ask you?" He asked.

"He wanted to know why we did not disclose our marriage to him at once. Also, he said he was advised by the other officers of what almost happened and apologized to me for general's inappropriate behavior. Even generals have rules they must abide by."

Iosif nodded. "Our commander is a decent man, and he will not let this incident rest. He said he has since warned the other base commanders, who have women stationed there, about the situation that almost happened."

"Did he tell you about the part where he will try to get us the necessary papers filed so that we will have documented proof of our marriage? He said it wasn't our fault the village we married in was destroyed. Or, it might just be simpler to have us remarry, now."

"Yes, yes he did." Iosef was so excited he did not see the smile on Sophie's face.

"Did the commander also ask you when our child was due?" She blinked a couple of times as she stared into his face.

"Oops," Iosif stopped. "Double oops! What did you tell him?"

"I told him I was not with child. That you misunderstood my stomach illness for pregnancy." Sophie started giggling like a young schoolgirl. "He also said you were a very clever officer and an honorable man. I think he knows we were never really married."

"I got that feeling as well, but he is going to make sure we are before the week is done."

Living up to his word, Sophie and Iosif were married by end of the week.

Chapter 18

Private Ulyana Obuchova hurried to the wooden house that had been erected for the women's mess hall. The air was crisp, and the sky was cloudless. "Look at you, sky. I have never seen you so blue." Ulyana smiled and twirled around looking up at the sky.

* * *

Vera sighed a long deep breath; she could not sleep. She sat at the edge of her cot and finally decided to head out to the mess hall. She began walking briskly when she spotted Ulyana. She was still baffled with Ulyana's child-like behavior. She was so naïve, trusting and positive about everything. Ulyana had told Vera that the flight training academy said she could not be a part of the flight crews. She pleaded with them to let her do something, so they gave her the kitchen detail, and she couldn't be happier.

"Comrade Ulyana, wait up," Vera called out to her. "I could not sleep, and I was chilled. I thought I would grab a cup of coffee and some bread." She sensed how proudly Ulyana stepped. "I have not been able to talk much with you these last few months. How are you faring in the kitchen?"

Ulyana spoke excitedly in her high pitched voice, "Oh, I love working there. The other two women are so kind and patient with me. I am not too smart and do not understand much, but I am learning very well they say."

"I am very glad to hear that," Vera looked up at Ulyana and walked faster to keep up with her long strides. "Comrade Ulyana, may I ask how tall you are?"

Ulyana nodded. Her deep brown, almost black eyes were sparkling. "Of course. The women in the kitchen also wanted to know this. They measured me to be six feet one inch tall." Her short, thin, brown hair blew around her boyish face.

"Thank you, comrade, I was just curious. They have constructed a nice mess hall for us," Vera said following her to the mess hall.

"Yes, we have not moved in a couple of weeks, and it makes it easier to get things done when you have a permanent place for them." She leaned down and whispered as if someone might hear her, "That is what the women tell me. They show me how to make cabbage soup, coffee and bread. I will be a great cook when I go home."

"I see," Vera said, smiling at the exuberance of the young woman.

"I wake up happy every morning that I am helping our Motherland in some way. Yes, it may be a very small way, but it brings me much joy."

"We need someone to feed us," Vera said. "So, it is a very necessary thing you do to help win this war."

"Yes, you are right. It is very necessary," she smiled broadly. "My boyfriend is also a kitchen helper at another base. I met him at a dance."

"Do you write to one another?"

"I am not such a good writer, but he is. I have the other two women read his letters to me, and then they write down what I want to say to him." She beamed, "I like him very much. One day, I will let him kiss me. Although, that thought does scare me a bit."

Vera held back her chuckle, "And why does that scare you a bit?"

"I have never been kissed before," she giggled. "He is very shy like me."

They entered the mess hall, and Ulyana took off her jacket and almost skipped to the kitchen area. "I must turn my record player on first. But do not worry the women make coffee for themselves early in the morning. I will get you a cup and some bread right away."

Soon Vera heard loud music coming from the kitchen and the two women who were in there with Ulyana laughing.

A little while later, Vera finished her coffee and bread. She waved good-bye to Ulyana, who was still singing cheerfully along with the record player, as she put fresh bread on the tables.

Vera left the mess hall feeling more refreshed. As she neared her quarters, something caught her eye in the sky. It was just a very small at first, and then she realized it was a plane. She hurried to the siren just in case it was an enemy plane. Then she spotted it. A Messerschmitt. She sounded the alarm and ran to her dugout to get her rifle.

Everyone peered out of their dugouts with their rifles ready to fire. The Messerschmitt began strafing the airplanes on the airfield and continued firing as he passed over the open field. As soon as the plane passed their dugouts the women came out and began firing their rifles and pistols. They all reloaded as quickly as they could and waited for the enemy plane to circle and come back for another strike. But it just kept flying until it was out of sight.

From what Vera could see, no one appeared to be hurt, and the only damage done was to two airplanes sitting on the airfield.

"Stinking fascist," Ksenia yelled.

"Over here!" A woman screamed from the mess hall. "Get a medic over here, quickly!"

Vera took off running to the mess hall and stopped at the door. On the floor in a pool of blood was the still body of Ulyana. A basket she had been holding with the breads was lying next to her on the floor. Her tall, thin frame was riddled with a spray of bullets.

"It happened so quickly," one of the women sobbed. "It happened so quickly. We did not hear any sirens or the plane coming. The music, she turned it up very loud today. I will break that record player. No more music. No more music." The two kitchen women held each other as they sobbed about the loss of their young helper.

Vera dropped to her knees by the lifeless body of the sweet, young girl. "When will this war ever end? I am so sick of the killing and dying." She wept openly for Ulyana. "She will never know a kiss." Vera spoke sadly to no one in particular.

Major Kashmir Korkavic rushed into the mess hall and pressed through the women standing around Ulyana lifeless body. "Oh, no" he said softly. "Not Ulyana." The major heaved a deep sigh. "We must grieve for our fallen comrade later. The German pilot will have radioed our location. We must leave immediately. I need all pilots who can fly, up in the air now, and find us a new airfield." He glanced down at Vera, "That means you, too."

Vera nodded and got up slowly. "Yes, Comrade Major." She did not look at anyone as she headed straight for her plane.

While the pilots were scouting out a new base headquarters, Major Korkavic wrote a letter to Ulyana's parents about their brave and dedicated daughter. He wrote to them telling them Ulyana was a true Citizen of the Soviet Union, and they should be honored by her selfless service.

A couple of weeks went by when the major called Vera into his headquarters. He sat there with a dejected face, as he handed Vera a letter from Ulyana's mother.

Vera began reading the letter and gave out a gasp. She felt for the chair behind her and fell into it. "This is true, Comrade Major?"

"Yes," Major Korkavic spoke sadly. "Ulyana was not her real name. It appears it was her older sister's name who had died at the age of two. Ulyana used her birth certificate to get into the Red Army; she was only twelve years old when she joined."

Vera's head shook. "That is why sometimes when I called her name she would not respond. Ulyana explained to me that it was because of all the excitement, and she was listening to too many other things. All this time I thought she was hiding a hearing problem."

"Now we know she did not respond because it was not her name. If she had not been so tall, we might have figured out her age before this tragic end." The major held out his hand for Vera to give him back the mother's letter. "We will keep this quiet for a while. I will see that she receives an honor bestowed on her posthumously. She worked hard and was proud to serve our Motherland. We could ask no more of her."

Vera was numb as she headed back to the large stone house the women were now being billeted in. All the women in the house had gone to the mess hall, except Ksenia.

Ksenia was sitting with her needlepoint and looked up at the distraught look on Vera's face. "Tell me, why the very long face? Tell me."

"How could this have happened? Why did we not pay more attention to signs that she was giving off? Vera walked over to their little kerosene stove and poured some old coffee into a cup. She turned and looked toward Ksenia.

"Something happened and we were not paying attention. She was giving off signs. Okay, I got that so far," Ksenia put down her needlepoint and folded her arms across her chest. "I will just sit here and wait until I can pay attention and not give off any signs."

Vera sat on her bed. "Dear God, the signs!"

"Signs? Stop right now and tell me what you are talking about." Ksenia demanded with frustration attacking every word.

Vera snapped out of her reverie and blurted out, "Ulyana was only twelve when she joined our regiment."

"What!" Ksenia yelled. "Twelve? Are they sure?"

"It appears that Ulyana stole her older sister's birth certificate, who died way before Ulyana was even born. Her birth certificate is what she used to get into the Army."

"Oh, God, the signs," Ksenia gasped. "I see what you mean. Like she had no idea about a woman having a 'visitor' on a monthly basis. We thought she was joking."

"She could not read or write very well at all and had no idea where a baby comes from," Vera exhaled sharply. "Again, I thought she was just fooling around when she talked about babies being found under a cabbage leaf. I thought, because she was so shy, that it was just an uncomfortable topic for her."

"Remember when she was afraid to go into the forest to get wood because she was afraid that Baba Yaga would get her," Ksenia uttered in amazement.

"That is a good one, but it does not count, because I have known some grown women who were afraid of Baba Yaga lurking about somewhere in the forest," Vera scoffed.

"Oh my, the swamp monster, Vodyanoy. You remember her fright when we had her go into the woods when all the snow melted making it look like a swamp. And we played off that scaring her even more," Ksenia lowered her head.

"I feel terrible about that now," Vera said sadly. "She was a child, just a child."

Both women sat in silence for a moment thinking of Ulyana, until Ksenia finally pulled herself together. "I will never think of her as a child, but a close friend that we came to love very dearly."

"Yes, I will do so as well," Vera leaned forward and nodded.

They sat quiet for a long time until Ksenia broke the silence.

Ksenia sniffled and wiped her nose with her blanket. "Well, Vera, we just did not think that a child, a very tall child, would be able to fool everyone, including us." Ksenia stretched her arms and yawned.

"You are right," Vera yawned, too. "Why is yawning so catchy? It is annoying. Now it is time for us to get ready to fly our sorties tonight, and I am yawning and beyond tired."

"I am always tired and yawning." Ksenia stood up, stretched and grabbed her jacket and leather cap. "At least it is warm weather now."

"Until we hit the higher altitudes, and then it is back to freezing again." Vera grabbed her things and headed out the door with Ksenia. "Let us see what the major has planned for us this night. I am sure it will take my mind of off Ulyana, for a little while."

The major had put down a large map that covered the table. "All of you get closer so I can show you what your sortie this evening will entail." Someone had drawn three circles on the map. There was a small circle in the center, a larger one surrounding it, and the third one was surrounding the other two.

"This looks like a dart board," Ksenia said looking at the strange circles on the map.

"These circles mark the placement of our soldiers and the Germans. The inner most circle, here in the middle of the map, is where our soldiers are being attacked by the Germans. The second circled area around it is where the Germans have entrenched themselves. The third circle is held by our regiments, surrounding the Germans. Does everyone understand this map?"

"Let me get this clear in my head, Comrade Major," Ksenia shook her head. "Our troops are in the inner most circle. The Germans have them surrounded, and we have the Germans surrounded. Is that it?"

"That is exactly it. This is going to be a joint effort with our fighters and bombers from the 586th and the 587th regiments, along with two other fighter regiments that will be accompanying you. The Germans have increased their fighters and bombers and are making a last attempt to break through our lines to take over the inner most circle," he said pointing to it.

"How did these three circles get to be three circles?" Vera asked.

"We believe their objective was to gain control of our ammunitions dump that is located in the first inner circle. They were not expecting us to come up behind them."

"But if we have them surrounded why are we not winning?" Vera asked.

"The Germans have heavy tanks, anti-aircraft cannons and ground missiles to take out our ground troops and aircraft. They have amped up their air forces as well. If they can break through to the inner circle where our troops are located, they will be able to capture our main ammunition center. They would then be able to combine our ammunition with theirs and have enough power to rip through our defenses, and we will have little to stop them."

"What is our objective?" Vera asked studying the three circles on the map.

"Your objectives are to blow up their tanks and ammunition dump and clear a path for our soldiers from the outer circle to help defend those caught in the inner center. You are going to come in from the east, and the 587th bombers are going to lead the attack accompanied by the 586th YAK fighters, and the two other fighter regiments. The 587th will be dropping their payloads first. They will fall back and help protect your planes so that you can make your drop. You are going to pass over our soldiers and head into the German held sector."

"The 587th has bombers that are bigger and can carry more payloads than our little ducklings. How soon after the PE-2s drop their payloads do we fly in? We will have to know because they do not fly as low as us, and we do not need the concussions from their bombs throwing our planes off course, or worse." Vera stood back from the map to study the layout better.

"Good question. The PE-2s will be the first wave in dropping their payloads. They have timed it so that when you fly your planes in at a lower altitude, it will be safe from any blowback from their bombs. The YAK-1 fighters will be flying along with them to help protect them from the fighters the Germans are going to throw at us. Once they have dropped their bombs you will fly in at a different angle and at a lower altitude. We must blow up their ammunition pile in order to bring them to their knees. This is going to be one of the most dangerous sorties you have made so far. Get yourselves ready for takeoff."

He looked at his watch. "It is 1800 hours now, and your take-off is at 1900 hours. You will rendezvous with all the other units at this location, quarter past the 1900 hour." He pointed to the designated meeting point. "For the Motherland."

The women responded, "For the Motherland."

"I want you to know that I have the finest pilots, navigators and ground crews in the entire Red Army. You have never ceased to amaze me – or the men. I think you have proven that you are brave and tenacious women who are to be looked up to and respected. Dismissed and good luck."

The pilots and navigators rushed to their planes and conferred with their ground crew to see if it was fueled and ready to fly. They checked their planes until they were satisfied it was in good enough condition to make the sortie.

Pilots, navigators and the ground crew were all assembled on the runway. They threw their arms around each other and wished each other luck. It was now a couple of minutes before1900 hours as they climbed into their planes; the propellers were wound, and their engines started. The flare went up for the first plane. It sped down the airfield and into the air, followed by all the other planes. They formed a straight line as they headed for their rendezvous point.

Chapter 19

Vera watched in awe, as they approached the Soviet planes filling the air space around them. There were YAK's, PE-2s and many other fighter planes that the Soviet Red Army had called up to stop the advancing German army.

They roared in unison as they flew toward the trapped Red Army unit. Vera had to wonder what those on the ground thought of the sky full of planes, all flying in the same direction, and close together. They must have looked like a swarm of locusts heading toward a feast.

There was no activity until they crossed over the territory where the Red Army had encircled the Germans.

Suddenly, the air was alive with German fighters as they swarmed in to attack the advancing Red Army planes. Several PE-2s pulled back and surrounded the little, unprotected, Biplanes that Vera and her regiment flew.

Vera and her regiment were nestled between the PE-2s. She looked over at the pilot of the PE-2 alongside of her plane and recognized Sophie. She pulled close to Vera's wing and waggled her plane. Then as quickly as Sophie's plane was next to her, it was gone.

* * *

"On their tail," Iosif yelled into his headset.

Sophie flipped her plane sideways and pulled a hard right. She came up alongside of a Messerschmitt as Iosif strafed it with his machine gun. "Got the Messer," he yelled. The enemy plane burst into flames and began to spiral downward.

"On your right," the radio operator yelled into his headset.

"You got it, Iosif?" Sophie yelled.

"Got it!" He screamed. There was a brilliant flash of light as the plane flying toward them on the right exploded.

"Our units are going in for the attack now," Sophie said into her headphone to the other fighter planes. "Prepare to cover these Biplanes."

The air was a mass of screaming engines and bullets flying as the Germans counter-attacked with a vengeance.

The closer the Soviets got to their target the fiercer the air battle became. YAKs assigned to protect them were drawn into a fight to the death as they tried to stave off any attacks on the weaponless Biplanes.

Bombs from the PE-2 bombers that could make it through the German air defense rained down devastation on the German forces below.

Anti-aircraft guns from both the Soviet and German side had to halt their cannons for fear of hitting one of their own.

The PE-2s moved over the Soviet troops and headed into German space. Everyone on this mission knew it was of upmost importance to take out the German ammunitions pile and destroy as many German tanks as possible along the way. The PE-2s did not make it in far enough to strike the ammunition dump, but they did manage to take out several tanks.

After they dropped their payloads, the PE-2s planes were lighter and more maneuverable in the air. They soon rejoined the fighter planes that were trying to make a pathway for the Biplanes.

* * *

Now it was up to Vera and her regiment to sneak in close enough to destroy the German ammunition dump. The YAKs and the powerful Ilyushin fighter planes moved in to protect them.

While the battle raged overhead, two by two, Vera's regiment flew in low over the Soviet battlefield. It was dark, and their only hope was that the sound of their engines would be hidden by the fierce air battle raging overhead.

It was anticipated that they would not be detected. The metal in their planes, and the heat from their engines was miniscule, and they were flying so low, that the German radar would not detect them.

Vera's face registered sheer terror as they flew in over the German-held ground. From the planes flying overhead fighting and lighting up the sky with their tracer bullets, and planes bursting into flames all around them, the entire sky was as brightly lit as if they were flying a daylight mission. Desperately, she tried to remember where the ammunition dump was on the map.

Then she spotted her target below. Suddenly, the anti aircraft guns came alive and began firing at them. Her plane was being violently jostled in the air from the concussions of the exploding flak that filled the air around her. Then, as suddenly as the anti-aircraft cannons had started, they stopped.

Off to the right, she saw a Messerschmitt coming right at them. She could do nothing but try to increase her speed and get to the ammo dump before it reached her.

The German pilot came in fast and low, firing its machine guns directly at her. Vera pulled her plane up fast and then dove down toward the ammunition dump. Bullets from the Messerschmitt swept across the tip of her wing as it flew past her, with a Soviet PE-2 right behind it. And, behind the PE-2, right on its tail was another Messerschmitt.

Vera knew she was not going to survive this sortie. Her luck had run out, and she thought it was probably inevitable. Her thoughts went to Yuri, and how much she loved him and was loved in return.

Machine guns, rifles and handguns were unloading at her from below, when suddenly an Ilyushin fighter pilot strafed the ground knocking out the shooters below. It climbed at incredible speed and took out the Messerschmitt following the PE-2.

Vera and the other Biplane pilots made their move and headed for the assigned targets: tanks and ammunition pile.

After they dropped their payloads, they immediately banked their planes to the right, and climbed higher to get out of reach of the concussion that was soon to follow. The force of the bombed ammunition dump blew their little planes sideways. They had managed to put enough distance from the explosion that it did not cause too much damage to their fragile planes.

Vera, and the other pilots, pushed their planes to the limit to get back into the safety net of the Soviet fighters. She glanced back to check on Ksenia, who smiled and gave her a thumbs-up. To her utter amazement, both were unhurt.

The aerial battle was almost over. She looked down in sadness at the splotches of fire sprinkled across the land. Vera knew it was the burning planes on both sides smoldering on the ground below. She wanted to scream, beat someone senseless, preferably Hitler, for starting this insane war, which caused the deaths of so many people – on all sides.

Her plane was hit several times. It shook and shuddered all the way back to base. Vera managed to make a safe landing and pulled their plane into its parking spot. She leaned back in the pilot's seat unable to move.

She watched as the other Biplanes came in for a landing. Vera counted the planes; two were missing. Her heart sank. She and her navigator came out of the sortie without a scratch, and yet four young women may have perished this day.

It took a while for Vera's legs to stop shaking, and when she felt she could finally walk; she climbed out of the cockpit and looked down at Ksenia, who was still sitting her cockpit. "Are you all right?" Vera asked concerned.

"Remember all the shaking and shuddering our plane was doing?" Ksenia asked as she stood up. "It was not the plane - it was me."

"Look," Vera pointed to the last plane to land. "It is Comrade Natalya's plane. She made it back as well. It is a good day."

Soon, the entire base was running down the runway laughing and jumping around as they came to see the flight crews.

Rimma and Larissa got to Vera and Ksenia hugging them and twirling them around.

"You made it!" Larissa cried excitedly.

"We did not think we would ever see you again." Rimma wiped away the tears running down her face. "So happy. So happy," was all she could say.

Vera smiled at the two mechanics. "We are happy, too, my friends."

"I notice that two planes did not come back with you," Larissa said. "But that does not mean that they are killed. We will not be sad until we know for certain what happened to them. Alright? Alright!"

"Yes, we have a big party for everyone's return." Rimma chortled.

"I am afraid I am not ready for a party," Ksenia shook her legs. "My legs are still trembling so badly; I do not think I can even make it back to our quarters."

"Have a solution for that problem," Rimma reached inside her jacket and pulled out a bottle of vodka. "This will help a great deal."

Ksenia's face lit up. "Well, now, that just may do the trick."

"You do not drink, Ksenia," Vera said laughing.

"I am going to start right now," she paused. "Well, how about we wait until I stop shaking. No need spilling the good stuff."

"Absolutely," Rimma said. "You rest. Then you drink a little."

"Deal," Ksenia said.

Natalya and Darya spotted Vera and Ksenia and ran to them hugging them and kissing them. "Comrades, you have survived as well."

"It was a good sight to see your plane land," Vera said hugging her again.

"Look who has come to say hello," Ksenia pointed toward the long strides of Katrina as she hurried toward them.

"You are all safe, my comrades," she took all four of them in a wide embrace. "Come, I have put coffee on and took some bread from the mess hall. I will put records on to play."

"Say this is getting better and better," Rimma said cheerfully.

"Especially since we are billeted in houses this time," Larissa chimed in. "We have more room to dance and on a better floor than a dirt one."

An hour later the door to their quarters opened, and Major Kashmir Korkavic walked in. "Comrades," he said. And before any of the women got up to salute him, he raised his hand to stop them. "Please do not get up. Katrina, please shut the music off for a moment."

Katrina immediately ran to the record player and shut it off.

"I wanted you to know that you took out the German ammunition pile, and the Germans have surrendered to our troops."

The women began screaming, laughing and hugging each other, until the major asked them to be quiet for a moment.

"I have canceled all sorties for tomorrow night. You deserve a day to rest and enjoy yourselves." The major smiled at the women as he left shutting the door behind him. "Good evening and enjoy your day tomorrow; and that is an order."

There was total quiet in the house. Everyone just sat there in stunned silence until Ksenia spoke, "Wow, that man is easy on the eyes. Can I take him home with me? Please?"

It brought shouts of laughter from everyone. The women were now jumping around laughing and hugging each other again.

They did not know that the major was still standing outside their quarters. He heard Ksenia and the women laughing inside and chuckled as he walked away.

Soon, everyone was up dancing and laughing for the rest of the night.

For the next whole day, the women played cards, wrote letters, read poetry, read books, played a little soccer, danced, napped, hung around talking or telling jokes or anything else they could think of to relax and enjoy the day.

On the following day, the women began their nightly sorties in the planes that could fly. They checked their maps and flew toward the location of the German encampment. As they reached their target area, there were no German bases, camps or soldiers to be seen anywhere. They circled around the area for miles to see if they had moved, but they were no enemy bases to be found. They flew back to their airfield and informed the major of their discovery.

Early the next morning Katrina woke everyone up. "The major has called a meeting outside of his main quarters. Everyone on base is to be present. Immediately."

All the women in the house grumbled. "Oh, do not tell me we have to fly recon over something. I am so tired from resting that if they had a mountain sitting on the ground, I would not see it." Natalya whined a little.

"Or worse, we have to carry another nasty, high-ranking officer to a far-off destination," Vera said yawning.

It was a warm morning as the women headed solemnly toward the meeting place.

The major nodded toward Katrina, which was her signal to speak. "All accounted for, Comrade Sr. Major Korkavic."

The major scanned all the women standing in front of him, took a deep breath and smiled. "I wanted all of you to know that the Germans are no longer here in the Soviet Union. They have withdrawn all their forces out of the Soviet Union. There have been reports that the Germans may be in talks to surrender."

It took a moment for the news to filter through everyone, and then they erupted into hysterical frenzy.

It took him a while to get everyone under control and quieted down so he could continue. "There are skirmishes in the Ukraine and Poland, but the German fronts are weak and easily defeated. There are thousands of German soldiers surrendering already."

The women began dancing and singing again, until Katrina barked for all of them to stop. "Our Comrade Major has more to say," she nodded for the major to continue.

"I just want to say that I have never been prouder than to have served as your base commander. You have accomplished so much and sacrificed so much. No matter where you go, no matter what walk of life you choose, you can hold your heads high and know you served your country well and bravely. I salute you." He raised his arm and saluted the women standing before him.

The women saluted him back and waited when he held his hand up for them to be still. "You will remain here until your papers come through releasing you from duty. I was told it was just a matter of a couple of days for some and longer for others." He smiled and shrugged. "Dismissed."

The major was not prepared for the onslaught of women as they rushed him and hugged and kissed him. Finally, Katrina pulled him from the excited women and escorted him back to his quarters where he had paperwork to complete before the women were evacuated.

"Comrade Katrina," the major touched her arm. "It was a lucky day for me when I inherited you as my assistant. You have been my right arm and a wonderful asset to me. Thank you for all of your help, Comrade Katrina."

"You have been a wonderful commander, and it is I that am thankful," she said humbly.

"Comrade Katrina, I do believe I hear a jeep headed this way," the major said.

"May I go Comrade Major," Katrina looked pleadingly at the major.

"With my blessings," he said saluting Katrina.

"Yes, Comrade Major," she saluted him back and raced out the door.

Chapter 20

Finally, the day came with the news that the war was indeed over, and everyone had their papers to either continue in the service or to become civilians. It would be a few more days before they would be transported back to Moscow. Major Korkavic had received his new orders and had flown out two days earlier.

The all-female regiments convened in a large, town hall that had not been damaged by the bombings. There was laughter and gaiety among the women, and yet, there was an undercurrent of sadness.

Vera spotted Sophie and moved through the throng of women to try to reach her. When Sophie saw Vera, she let out a holler and grabbed her, hugging and kissing her cheeks. "You made it, Comrade Vera."

"Thanks to you," Vera said with tears forming in her eyes.

"Not just me, but all of these women had participated. Like her." She pointed to a tall, brown-haired woman talking with another pilot. "On our joint major offensive, she was flying an Ilyushin and shot down the Messer that was chasing me and kept numerous Messer's from shooting your group down. Fantastic pilot."

"How did your all-male crew do?" Vera asked.

"They all survived, but I had to punish one of them severely though," she said shaking her head.

"What did you do to him?"

"I married him." Both women laughed heartily.

"I do hope we will stay in touch," Vera said wiping a tear from her eyes from the laughing.

"We must," Sophie spoke with sincerity.

"Well, we are all here. Let us try to work something out," Vera walked with Sophie to the front of the hall where a speaker's podium was located.

"Comrades, may I have your attention, please," Vera yelled over the din in the room.

"Comrades," Sophie yelled even louder.

The noise finally subsided as the two women looked out over the faces of their comrades.

"We would like to propose that we all stay in touch," Vera said.

"Suggestions on how we can do that are up for discussion," Sophie spoke loudly to the quiet group of women before her.

Finally, after many suggestions and debates, it was Katrina's idea that met with approval from everyone. Each year on May 2, they would meet in a small park across from the Bolshoi theater in Moscow.

Vera located Larissa and Rimma and gave them both a hug and kiss on each cheek. "I am so glad that you two were my mechanics. Ksenia and I were very lucky. As far as I am concerned, I had the best mechanics in the regiment. Thank you for all of your hard work." Vera stopped a tear from rolling down her cheek.

"Now stop that," Rimma's voice started to quiver. "You are a great pilot and Ksenia a great navigator. We are the ones who consider ourselves lucky."

"I will second that," Larissa nodded and smiled.

"Hey," Ksenia hollered, walking up to her three friends. "How is the best team on the planet doing?"

"We were just discussing how lucky we were to be assigned to each other," Vera nodded to the two mechanics.

"I will agree with that completely," Ksenia laughed and then waved for Maria and Zoya to join them.

The two women approached Ksenia and her small group. After they had made their introductions, Sophie ambled over to the group.

"I see you have met my top-notch mechanics," Sophie hugged Maria and Zoya.

"Yes, and I want you to meet mine," Vera laughed and introduced Rimma and Larissa.

"I have been talking to a lot of mechanics, and I can attest that they were all pretty great." Larissa said.

"We all went through the same thing, and it was not easy for any of us," Rimma stated firmly.

"And it certainly was not easy for you pilots and navigators either," Maria responded quickly.

"I will miss all of you very much," Larissa spoke sadly.

"In one year, we will be all together again," Zoya smiled, but there was sadness in her eyes.

"One year. I will be there," Vera said emphatically to the women she had come to love. "Okay, enough of this or I will be crying all day. I wish you could have met Natalya. She was a pilot, and a great poet. She and her navigator, Darya, left early this morning. They are returning to the university to finish their studies."

Vera spotted Katrina and motioned for her to join them. "You must meet one of the cleverest assistants in our division. We don't know what we would have done without here."

Katrina smiled, introduced herself and talked with them for a while. "I am very pleased to have met all of you, but I must leave now as I am expecting to meet up with the love of my life; Georgie." She began walking toward the door.

"Wait up," Vera said. "I'll walk with you."

"Oh, my. That woman has the most beautiful hair I have ever seen," Zoya said staring after Katrina.

"Very pretty girl and truly fantastic hair," Maria quipped.

Soon, Rimma, Larissa, Maria and Zoya began talking in their own little group when Zoya asked Rimma, "Why do you look so sad? The war is over and now we have peace."

"She is happy about that," Larissa said, "but she is sad because her beau is gone."

"He was killed? I am so sorry," Maria exclaimed.

"No, he is not dead," Rimma spoke softly. "He left a couple of days ago, and I have not heard from him since he left."

"She did not miss him before," Larissa cocked her head and looked at Rimma.

"I did not know how much I really cared for him until he left," she said sadly. "He did not even say good-bye. It was probably just a wartime romance for him."

Larissa raised her eyebrows at Zoya and Maria, who seemed genuinely concerned, "She shot him down more than our Ace pilots shot down the Germans. And now she is wondering why he left without saying good-bye."

"Sorry, about that," Zoya smiled weakly.

"Let us not talk about me," Rimma put on her best smile. "I want to hear all about what you two are going to be doing now that the war is over."

The four women began to talk and laugh among themselves and were quickly joined by other mechanics. The next couple of hours the women mingled with each other, introducing themselves and describing what part they played during the war, and what they were going to do now.

Vera was standing outside talking with other pilots when they heard a plane heading in their direction. As it got closer, they could make out the shape of the plane. "It is one of our planes," Vera relaxed her stance.

The plane taxied up the grassy field toward them, getting as close to the town hall as it could. A tall, handsome man in a Soviet Union uniform stepped out causing a lot of oh's and ah's from the women standing outside.

"Comrade Major Kashmir Korkavic?" Vera exclaimed.

He walked up to the women standing in front of the town hall. Katrina knew exactly who he was looking for and nodded her head toward the doorway. "You will find what you are looking for inside."

Everyone followed him in through the door. He stopped for a moment and spotted exactly where he was going. Rimma had her back to him as he walked up behind her. "Comrade Senior Sergeant Rimma Trovitz, I have a question for you," he blurted out.

Rimma whirled around in surprise when she heard the major's voice, "The answer is yes."

He continued, "I will not take no for an..." It took a minute for it to register, and he broke into a huge smile. "Then we must leave now; all the paperwork has been filed, and we can be married immediately." He took her hand, and they hurried out of the town hall to the plane still idling on the grass. Rimma waved happily to her friends as she got into the plane.

"It is time for Zoya, Maria and I to leave as well," Sophie said. "But now we know this is not good-bye forever; we will see each other next year."

The women said their good-byes and left to their designated bases to await further orders, leaving Vera and her regiment alone in the town hall.

They began talking to one another when the beeping of a jeep horn diverted their attention.

"Oh, that is my Georgie coming to pick me up. They are sending me to his base to be an assistant to the base commander in a town called Ryazan. We have decided after we are officially discharged, we are going to finish our degrees in Agriculture, so we can better help the collective farm of my parents."

Corporal Georgie Spokva pulled abruptly up in front of them. "I have come to pick up my wife."

"I must go, now." Katrina giggled and waved to Georgie in the jeep.

"Did I hear him say something about a wife?" Vera asked folding her arms in front of her.

"Yes," Katrina's pretty face lit up. "We were married last night."

"Come on," Georgie yelled. "Time to get going."

"I shall miss all of you dearly. But we will all meet in one year, and I shall look forward to it all year." Katrina hugged and kissed everyone and jumped into the front seat next to her new husband.

Georgie peeled the jeep around and sped away with Katrina waving until her husband pulled her close to him putting his arm around her shoulders.

"She certainly has the most beautiful hair - ever," Ksenia and Vera said at the same time, and then broke into laughter.

One by one everyone said their good-byes until it was only Vera, Ksenia and Larissa left from their regiment.

They walked quietly back to the house. It had been warm all day, but a cold wind began to blow as the night crept closer. It would be dark soon, so they quickly scurried around to find some firewood.

Soon, a roaring fire filled the room with warmth. "Well, with everyone gone but us we can pull our beds closer to the fire."

"Just so you know I will be leaving at the break of day," Larissa said. "I have been assigned as a mechanics instructor," she paused and rolled her eyes happily, "to an all-male regiment. Seems my reputation as a great mechanic precedes me."

"That is wonderful, Larissa." Vera stretched her hands closer to the fire. "What have you finally decided, Ksenia?" Vera queried.

Ksenia leaned back against the wall. "I have decided to stay in the service for a while. I was asked if I would come to the Engels training school and instruct for a while. They want me to be a test pilot as well with all the new planes they have been making. Actually, I was trained to be a pilot before they made me your navigator."

"What about you and your plans, Vera?" Ksenia asked.

"My orders give me a week's leave, and I am going to use that to find Yuri." Vera leaned her head back against the wall. "I have not heard from him in a while, and I am very worried about him."

"She got letters from him, but the dates were a few months behind," Ksenia said.

"That is just a normal part of being on the move all the time," Larissa shrugged. "It is not that his letters are late; it is the letters trying to find you."

"Yes, I believe that as well," Vera said. "So, right now let us enjoy each other's company."

"Agreed," Ksenia and Larissa said at the same time.

The three women laughed and reminisced until they became so tired, they fell asleep. When they awoke in the morning, Larissa had already left.

"Well, we are the last of our regiment to leave. I will be leaving right after our morning meal. When do you leave?" Ksenia asked Vera.

"About the same time, or a little later. I was told someone would be here to pick me up a little after our breakfast."

Vera and Ksenia made coffee in the old fireplace, ate their stale bread, and talked until they heard the truck for Ksenia pull up to their house.

Vera cried so hard when Ksenia was leaving, she thought she would never straighten herself out. Ksenia had gotten to the truck and had asked them to wait. She ran back and gave Vera another big hug, sobbing just as hard as Vera.

Alone for the first time, Vera walked around the room she had shared with her friends. She looked at each cot and could see her friends. Those that had died and those that had survived were all ghosts before her. She could see them writing letters, reading, laughing and dancing around the room.

For more than three years, they lived side by side sharing their joys, sadness, terrors, pains and laugher. It seemed like they would never be apart; that they would always be together to share everything. It did not occur to her that their being together would ever end. They became a family. They were part of her and would always be a part of her.

She heard the rumble of a jeep, far off, driving down the dirt road. Sighing and taking one last look at the empty room, she walked out the door, saying good-bye forever.

Vera slung her duffle bag over her shoulder and shut the door behind her. Her eyes were downcast, and her heart filled with almost unbearable sadness. The misty, morning air swirled around her as she began to walk down the road to meet the jeep. She pulled her jacket tightly to her against the cold morning air and glanced over at the mist covered field across the road.

Memories flooded her mind and filled her heart with the thoughts of her comrades who had fallen. For a brief instant, she thought she saw Elena and Nikolai with their arms around each other smiling and waving at her from within the mist.

Without thinking she smiled and raised her hand waving back at them. Vera looked down the road at the approaching jeep, and when she looked back, the images of Elena and Nikolai had faded away.

The jeep pulled up to her, and Vera threw her duffle bag in the back seat as she climbed in. As the jeep pulled away Vera glanced back at the house she and her comrades were billeted in, and then over at the grassy airfield where their fragile, little Biplanes once sat.

But now her thoughts were on finding Yuri, and the future with him, as they traveled down the dusty road toward the last place he had been stationed. The closer they got to the village the more traffic appeared in the road.

Vera had been riding for a couple of hours and did not pay any attention to a jeep on the other side of the road that had come to a screeching halt and made a U-turn.

The soldier, who was driving Vera, stopped at the base headquarters stationed in the small village. Vera got out of the jeep to stretch her legs, when she spotted a hospital tent. She thought maybe someone in the tent would know Yuri, and hopefully know where he was stationed.

As she walked toward the tent, a jeep pulled up behind her. The driver threw open the door and raced toward Vera. "Vera," he called out.

Vera turned around and was stunned to see Yuri coming toward her. She ran into his arms crying and laughing at the same time.

"Vera, my dearest," he held her so tightly she could barely breath, and she didn't care.

"How did you find me?" Vera asked still holding him.

He pulled away and began stroking her wet cheeks. "After the war ended, I asked for a leave, but it was denied. I was on the front lines, and the wounded were pouring in. It took them a while to transfer the patients to proper hospitals, and when they felt I was no longer necessary I got a two-day leave." He took her face and held it in his hands.

"But how did you know I would be on this road?" She asked puzzled.

"It was the strangest and the most wonderful accident that I found you at all," he laughed as he stroked her hair. "This town is called Ryazan where I have been working with the wounded. When I got my two days leave, I asked the base commander if he knew where the 588th regiment was quartered. He said he had no idea when a young woman, with exceptionally beautiful hair, said she knew exactly where they were, and even more incredible she got me this jeep. She had it filled with fuel and told me to go and get you."

"But... but how..." Vera stammered in disbelief that they had managed to meet.

"I was on my way to get you when I saw you sitting in a jeep going the other way," he pulled her to him again and gently took her in his arms. "Now, we shall be together forever. It will be just the two of us from now on."

Vera whispered into his ear, "No, it will be the three of us."

"What?" Yuri whirled her around laughing and kissing her. "This is wonderful." He put her down and held her tightly to him.

Vera looked up into Yuri's face and saw the love pouring from his eyes. The past would always be a part of her. It was a journey she had taken that would always hold memories of war, laughter, terror, pain, but most importantly - friendships.

Now she was embarking on another journey; a journey of love, hope and peace.

Epilogue

The surviving women of the 586th, 587th and 588th met in a park across from the Bolshoi theater. Every year, the women who could, met as they had promised. There were tears, laughter and dancing. Those that could, came with their husbands, children and grandchildren to have them share in their memories. They proudly wore their medals on their blouses or jackets.

Vera, Yuri and their five children went every year to the reunion, except for one time, she was in labor and missed the day. She stayed in touch with Ksenia throughout the years by phone or letters. And every year Ksenia and her family of four reunited with Vera on May 2.

Natalya had become a famous engineer but was far more famous as a poet. Her husband and children had been killed during the war, and she never remarried. But every year she showed up at the reunion. Her navigator, Darya, married and moved too far away to make all the reunions; although she managed to make it to the fortieth reunion.

Rimma was happily married to the major, and they had four children, and two grandchildren.

Larissa married a mechanic she met when she was transferred at the end of the war. They had three children and one grandchild.

Sophie and Iosef moved to Paris, with their two children, one grandchild and Sophie's younger brother and sister. They were still happily making each other crazy. But Sophie made sure she would be back for the fortieth reunion.

Zoya returned to the factory and married a fellow worker and had no children.

Maria married a man a foot shorter than her, and they had six children of various heights.

Katrina and Georgie finished their Agricultural degrees and helped her parents out on the Collective Farm. Katrina bore Georgie nine children, and they had fourteen grandchildren.

When all the women met again after forty years, there was so much screaming and crying it began to draw a crowd.

Katrina started the dancing, and soon all the women were dancing and laughing as they sang songs from long ago.

* * *

Several teenagers were walking near the Bolshoi theatre and spotted several older women dancing and singing in a park nearby. Out of curiosity, they walked over to see what was going on.

"What are those crazy old ladies dancing and singing for?" A young man with unruly brown hair asked.

"What are those badges on their blouses?" A young girl asked.

"No, they're not badges. They look like medals," another girl said.

"From doing what, washing clothes or scrubbing floors to perfection," laughed another young man.

Yuri was standing near them and shook his head. He walked over to the four teenagers laughing at the women he had come to love and respect. "Yes, those are medals won by all of those incredible women. They earned them in World War II. If you look closely you will even see the Hero of the Soviet Union medals on most of their blouses."

"What? What could women do during World War II to earn them the Hero of the Soviet Union?" the teen boy said laughing in disbelief.

"They flew planes dropping bombs on Germans at night, with no weapons to protect themselves. They flew fighter planes against the seasoned Luftwaffe and won many an air battle. There were three Soviet women Aces during that war. These amazing women would fly toward death every day with bravery and honor. Some of those women were the ground crews who worked out in the open with no protection from the weather or insects. Their living conditions were appalling, and they never complained. They fought and died so that you would not be living under Nazi control. That is how these amazing women earned their medals."

"That is incredible," said one of the girls as they walked away.

"You believe that, Katyana?" The young man with the unruly hair said. "If it was true how come we have never heard about them? They do not mention it in any of our history classes."

"I believe what he said, Oleg. Women are capable of many great things, just like men," snapped Katyana. She stopped, turned, and smiled as she watched the older women laughing and dancing. "They flew toward death every day with bravery and honor; that is what he said."

"Katyana," yelled Oleg. "Come on, we are waiting for you."

"You go ahead; I want to meet these women," Katyana waved to her friends and headed back to the women of the Red Army all-female regiments.

The End

Dear reader,

We hope you enjoyed reading *Fly Toward Death*. Please take a moment to leave a review, even if it's a short one. Your opinion is important to us.

Discover more books by Sally Laughlin at
https://www.nextchapter.pub/authors/sally-laughlin

Want to know when one of our books is free or discounted? Join the newsletter at http://eepurl.com/bqqB3H

Best regards,
Sally Laughlin and the Next Chapter Team

Postscript

This book, although fictional, gives a brief glimpse into what their lives were *really* like during World War II.

An average age of the pilots, navigators, ground and armament crews were between seventeen and twenty-six years old. Not only were flying conditions harsh, so were the living conditions along with having to deal with sexual harassment and a great deal of skepticism.

There were three all-female regiments:

The 588th was the most highly decorated female unit in the Soviet Air Force. Their "job" was to harass the German army by bombing them at night, in a biplane that was used in World War I. It was made of balsam wood and canvas, with no weapons to protect themselves. The 588th regiment flew over 23,000 sorties and dropped over 3,000 tons of bombs and 26,000 incendiary shells. They began their flights starting at dusk and ending at dawn. It was a continual loop: drop their bombs, return to base to get two more bombs and back in the air to drop another pay load. The 588th later became :46th Taman Guards Night Bomber Aviation Regiment to honor their bravery and flying accomplishments. The Germans were so terrorized by these women fliers the offered a reward to any pilot that shot one day of 2,000 Marks and an Iron Cross.

The 587th were the ПЕ2 Dive Bombers (Petlyakov 2). It was a solid bomber, fighter and reconnaissance plane. It was a complex aircraft that carried a 1,000 kg bomb load and a crew of three: pilot, navigator-bombardier and tail-gunner. The 587th regiment was later called the 125th Guards Dive Bomber Regiment. Later, men were slowly integrated into the all-female unit. They flew 1,134 missions and dropped over 980 tons of bombs.

The 586th were a defense regiment. Its primary duty was to guard important targets from enemy bombers and to escort aircraft of important persons. They flew the Yak 1 fighter (Yakovlev 1). They were to protect cities, airfields and any important transportation vehicles from enemy attacks. They completed more than 9,000 flights and flew 4,419 combat sorties.

Reported statistics: 1,000 women joined the Soviet air defense, and 300 or more were killed.

These are the statistics put out by the Soviet Union.

About the Author

Currently, I am happily living in northern Ohio with my sane sister, nutty dog and brat cat.

Fly Toward Death
ISBN: 978-4-86752-133-5

Published by
Next Chapter
1-60-20 Minami-Otsuka
170-0005 Toshima-Ku, Tokyo
+818035793528
26th July 2021